Clive Barker was born in Liverpool in 1952. He is the author of The Books of Blood (in six volumes), The Damnation Game, Weaveworld, Cabal, The Great and Secret Show, Imajica and Everville.

He also writes, directs and produces for the screen. His films include Hellraiser and Nightbreed.

He lives in Los Angeles.

Also by Clive Barker:

Clive Barker's Books of Blood

volume VI

CLIVE BARKER

Every body is a book of blood;
Wherever we're opened, we're red.

WARNER BOOKS

A *Warner* Book

First published in Great Britain in 1985 by Sphere Books
Reprinted 1986, 1987, 1988, 1989, 1990, 1991, 1993
Reprinted by Warner Books 1994

ISBN 0 7221 1375 7

Printed in England by Clays Ltd, St Ives plc

Sphere Books
A Division of
Macdonald & Co (Publishers)
Brettenham House
Lancaster Place
London WC2E 7EN

To Dave

CONTENTS

THE LIFE OF DEATH

THE NEWSPAPER WAS the first edition of the day, and Elaine devoured it from cover to cover as she sat in the hospital waiting room. An animal thought to be a panther – which had terrorised the neighbourhood of Epping Forest for two months – had been shot and found to be a wild dog. Archaeologists in the Sudan had discovered bone fragments which they opined might lead to a complete reappraisal of Man's origins. A young woman who had once danced with minor royalty had been found murdered near Clapham; a solo round-the-world yachtsman was missing; recently excited hopes of a cure for the common cold had been dashed. She read the global bulletins and the trivia with equal fervour – anything to keep her mind off the examination ahead – but today's news seemed very like yesterday's; only the names had been changed.

Doctor Sennett informed her that she was healing well, both inside and out, and was quite fit to return to her full responsibilities whenever she felt psychologically resilient enough. She should make another appointment for the first week of the new year, he told her, and come back for a final examination then. She left him washing his hands of her.

The thought of getting straight onto the bus and heading back to her rooms was repugnant after so much time sitting and waiting. She would walk a stop or two along the route, she decided. The exercise would be good for her, and the December day, though far from warm, was bright.

Her plans proved over-ambitious however. After only a few minutes of walking her lower abdomen began to ache, and she started to feel nauseous, so she turned off the main road to seek out a place where she could rest and drink some tea. She should eat too, she knew, though she had never had much appetite, and had less still since the operation. Her wanderings were rewarded. She found a small restaurant which, though it was twelve fifty-five, was not enjoying a roaring lunch-time trade. A small woman with unashamedly artificial red hair served her tea and a mushroom omelette. She did her best to eat, but didn't get very far. The waitress was plainly concerned.

'Something wrong with the food?' she said, somewhat testily.

'Oh no,' Elaine reassured her. 'It's just me.'

The waitress looked offended nevertheless.

'I'd like some more tea though, if I may?' Elaine said.

She pushed the plate away from her, hoping the waitress would claim it soon. The sight of the meal congealing on the patternless plate was doing nothing for her mood. She hated this unwelcome sensitivity in herself: it was absurd that a plate of uneaten eggs should bring these doldrums on, but she couldn't help herself. She found everywhere little echoes of her own loss. In the death, by a benign November and then the sudden frosts, of the bulbs in her window-sill box; in the thought of the wild dog she'd read of that morning, shot in Epping Forest.

The waitress returned with fresh tea, but failed to take the plate. Elaine called her back, requesting that she do so. Grudgingly, she obliged.

There were no customers left in the place now, other than Elaine, and the waitress busied herself with removing the lunchtime menus from the tables and replacing them with those for the evening. Elaine sat staring out of the window. Veils of blue-grey smoke had crept down the street in recent minutes, solidifying the sunlight.

'They're burning again,' the waitress said. 'Damn smell gets everywhere.'

'What are they burning?'

'Used to be the community centre. They're knocking it down, and building a new one. It's a waste of tax-payers' money.'

The smoke was indeed creeping into the restaurant. Elaine did not find it offensive; it was sweetly redolent of autumn, her favourite season. Intrigued, she finished her tea, paid for her meal, and then elected to wander along and find the source of the smoke. She didn't have far to walk. At the end of the street was a small square; the demolition site dominated it. There was one surprise however. The building that the waitress had described as a community centre was in fact a church; or had been. The lead and slates had already been stripped off the roof, leaving the joists bare to the sky; the windows had been denuded of glass; the turf had gone from the lawn at the side of the building, and two trees had been felled

3

there. It was their pyre which provided the tantalising scent.

She doubted if the building had ever been beautiful, but there was enough of its structure remaining for her to suppose it might have had charm. Its weathered stone was now completely at variance with the brick and concrete that surrounded it, but its besieged situation (the workmen labouring to undo it; the bulldozer on hand, hungry for rubble) gave it a certain glamour.

One or two of the workmen noticed her standing watching them, but none made any move to stop her as she walked across the square to the front porch of the church and peered inside. The interior, stripped of its decorative stonework, of pulpit, pews, font and the rest, was simply a stone room, completely lacking in atmosphere or authority. Somebody, however, had found a source of interest here. At the far end of the church a man stood with his back to Elaine, staring intently at the ground. Hearing footsteps behind him he looked round guiltily.

'Oh,' he said. 'I won't be a moment.'

'It's all right –' Elaine said. 'I think we're probably both trespassing.'

The man nodded. He was dressed soberly – even drearily – but for his green bow-tie. His features, despite the garb and the grey hairs of a man in middle-age, were curiously unlined, as though neither smile nor frown much ruffled their perfect indifference.

'Sad, isn't it?' he said. 'Seeing a place like this.'

'Did you know the church as it used to be?'

'I came in on occasion,' he said, 'but it was never very popular.'

'What's it called?'

'All Saints. It was built in the late seventeenth century, I believe. Are you fond of churches?'

'Not particularly. It was just that I saw the smoke, and . . .'

'Everybody likes a demolition scene,' he said.

'Yes,' she replied, 'I suppose that's true.'

'It's like watching a funeral. Better them than us, eh?'

She murmured something in agreement, her mind flitting elsewhere. Back to the hospital. To her pain and her present healing. To her life saved only by losing the capacity for further life. *Better them than us.*

'My name's Kavanagh,' he said, covering the short distance between them, his hand extended.

'How do you do?' she said. 'I'm Elaine Rider.'

'Elaine,' he said. 'Charming.'

'Are you just taking a final look at the place before it comes down?'

'That's right. I've been looking at the inscriptions on the floor stones. Some of them are most eloquent.' He brushed a fragment of timber off one of the tablets with his foot. 'It seems such a loss. I'm sure they'll just smash the stones to smithereens when they start to pull the floor up –'

She looked down at the patchwork of tablets beneath her feet. Not all were marked, and of those that were many simply carried names and dates. There were some inscriptions however. One, to the left of where Kavanagh was standing, carried an all but eroded relief of crossed shin-bones, like drum-sticks, and the abrupt motto: *Redeem the time.*

'I think there must have been a crypt under here at some time,' Kavanagh said.

'Oh. I see. And these are the people who were buried there.'

'Well, I can't think of any other reason for the inscriptions, can you? I was thinking of asking the work-

5

men . . .' he paused in mid-sentence, '. . . you'll probably think this positively morbid of me . . .'

'What?'

'Well, just to preserve one or two of the finer stones from being destroyed.'

'I don't think that's morbid,' she said. 'They're very beautiful.'

He was evidently encouraged by her response. 'Maybe I should speak with them now,' he said. 'Would you excuse me for a moment?'

He left her standing in the nave like a forsaken bride, while he went out to quiz one of the workmen. She wandered down to where the altar had been, reading the names as she went. Who knew or cared about these people's resting places now? Dead two hundred years and more, and gone away not into loving posterity but into oblivion. And suddenly the unarticulated hopes for an after-life she had nursed through her thirty-four years slipped away; she was no longer weighed down by some vague ambition for heaven. One day, perhaps *this* day, she would die, just as these people had died, and it wouldn't matter a jot. There was nothing to come, nothing to aspire to, nothing to dream of. She stood in a patch of smoke-thickened sun, thinking of this, and was almost happy.

Kavanagh returned from his exchanges with the foreman.

'There is indeed a crypt,' he said, 'but it hasn't been emptied yet.'

'Oh.'

They were still underfoot, she thought. Dust and bones.

'Apparently they're having some difficulty getting into it. All the entrances have been sealed up. That's

6

why they're digging around the foundations. To find another way in.'

'Are crypts normally sealed up?'

'Not as thoroughly as this one.'

'Maybe there was no more room,' she said.

Kavanagh took the comment quite seriously. 'Maybe,' he said.

'Will they give you one of the stones?'

He shook his head. 'It's not up to them to say. These are just council lackeys. Apparently they have a firm of professional excavators to come in and shift the bodies to new burial sites. It all has to be done with due decorum.'

'Much they care,' Elaine said, looking down at the stones again.

'I must agree,' Kavanagh replied. 'It all seems in excess of the facts. But then perhaps we're not God-fearing enough.'

'Probably.'

'Anyhow, they told me to come back in a day or two's time, and ask the removal men.'

She laughed at the thought of the dead moving house; packing up their goods and chattels. Kavanagh was pleased to have made a joke, even if it had been unintentional. Riding on the crest of this success, he said: 'I wonder, may I take you for a drink?'

'I wouldn't be very good company, I'm afraid,' she said. 'I'm really very tired.'

'We could perhaps meet later,' he said.

She looked away from his eager face. He was pleasant enough, in his uneventful way. She liked his green bow-tie – surely a joke at the expense of his own drabness. She liked his seriousness too. But she couldn't face the idea of drinking with him; at least not tonight. She made her apologies, and explained

7

that she'd been ill recently and hadn't recovered her stamina.

'Another night perhaps?' he enquired gently. The lack of aggression in his courtship was persuasive, and she said:

'That would be nice. Thank you.'

Before they parted they exchanged telephone numbers. He seemed charmingly excited by the thought of their meeting again; it made her feel, despite all that had been taken from her, that she still had her sex.

She returned to the flat to find both a parcel from Mitch and a hungry cat on the doorstep. She fed the demanding animal, then made herself some coffee and opened the parcel. In it, cocooned in several layers of tissue paper, she found a silk scarf, chosen with Mitch's uncanny eye for her taste. The note along with it simply said: *It's your colour. I love you. Mitch.* She wanted to pick up the telephone on the spot and talk to him, but somehow the thought of hearing his voice seemed dangerous. Too close to the hurt, perhaps. He would ask her how she felt, and she would reply that she was well, and he would insist: yes, but *really*? And she would say: I'm empty; they took out half my innards, damn you, and I'll never have your children or anybody else's, so that's the end of that, isn't it? Even thinking about their talking she felt tears threaten, and in a fit of inexplicable rage she wrapped the scarf up in the desiccated paper and buried it at the back of her deepest drawer. Damn him for trying to make things better now, when at the time she'd most needed him all he'd talked of was fatherhood, and how her tumours would deny it him.

It was a clear evening – the sky's cold skin stretched to breaking point. She did not want to draw the curtains in the front room, even though passers-by would stare in, because the deepening blue was too fine to miss. So she sat at the window and watched the dark come. Only when the last change had been wrought did she close off the chill.

She had no appetite, but she made herself some food nevertheless, and sat down to watch television as she ate. The food unfinished, she laid down her tray, and dozed, the programmes filtering through to her intermittently. Some witless comedian whose merest cough sent his audience into paroxysms; a natural history programme on life in the Serengeti; the news. She had read all that she needed to know that morning: the headlines hadn't changed.

One item, however, did pique her curiosity: an interview with the solo yachtsman, Michael Maybury, who had been picked up that day after two weeks adrift in the Pacific. The interview was being beamed from Australia, and the contact was bad; the image of Maybury's bearded and sun-scorched face was constantly threatened with being snowed out. The picture mattered little: the account he gave of his failed voyage was riveting in sound alone, and in particular an event that seemed to distress him afresh even as he told it. He had been becalmed, and as his vessel lacked a motor had been obliged to wait for wind. It had not come. A week had gone by with his hardly moving a kilometre from the same spot of listless ocean; no bird or passing ship broke the monotony. With every hour that passed, his claustrophobia grew, and on the eighth day it reached panic proportions, so he let himself over the side of the yacht and swam away from the vessel, a life-line tied about his middle, in order to escape the same few yards of deck. But once away from the yacht, and treading the still, warm water, he had no desire to go back. Why not untie the knot, he'd thought to himself, and float away.

'What made you change your mind?' the interviewer asked.

Here Maybury frowned. He had clearly reached the crux of his story, but didn't want to finish it. The interviewer repeated the question.

At last, hesitantly, the sailor responded. 'I looked back at the yacht,' he said, 'and I saw somebody on the deck.'

The interviewer, not certain that he'd heard correctly, said: 'Somebody on the deck?'

'That's right,' Maybury replied. 'Somebody was there. I saw a figure quite clearly; moving around.'

'Did you . . . did you recognise this stowaway?' the question came.

Maybury's face closed down, sensing that his story was being treated with mild sarcasm.

'Who was it?' the interviewer pressed.

'I don't know,' Maybury said. 'Death, I suppose.'

The questioner was momentarily lost for words.

'But of course you returned to the boat, eventually.'

'Of course.'

'And there was no sign of anybody?'

Maybury glanced up at the interviewer, and a look of contempt crossed his face.

'I've survived, haven't I?' he said.

The interviewer mumbled something about not understanding his point.

'I didn't drown,' Maybury said. 'I could have died then, if I'd wanted to. Slipped off the rope and drowned.'

'But you didn't. And the next day –'

'The next day the wind picked up.'

'It's an extraordinary story,' the interviewer said, content that the stickiest part of the exchange was now safely by-passed. 'You must be looking forward to seeing your family again for Christmas . . .'

Elaine didn't hear the final exchange of pleasantries. Her imagination was tied by a fine rope to the room she was sitting in; her fingers toyed with the knot. If Death could find a boat in the wastes of the Pacific, how much easier it must be to find her. To sit with her, perhaps, as she slept. To watch her as she went about her mourning. She stood up and turned the television off. The flat was suddenly silent. She questioned the hush impatiently, but it held no sign of guests, welcome or unwelcome.

As she listened, she could taste salt-water. Ocean, no doubt.

She had been offered several refuges in which to convalesce when she came out of hospital. Her father had invited her up to Aberdeen; her sister Rachel had made several appeals for her to spend a few weeks in Buckinghamshire; there had even been a pitiful telephone call from Mitch, in which he had talked of their holidaying together. She had rejected them all, telling them that she wanted to re-establish the rhythm of her previous life as soon as possible: to return to her job, to her working colleagues and friends. In fact, her reasons had gone deeper than that. She had *feared* their sympathies, feared that she would be held too close in their affections and quickly come to rely upon them. Her streak of independence, which had first brought her to this unfriendly city, was in studied defiance of her smothering appetite for security. If she gave in to those loving appeals she knew she would take root in domestic soil and not look up and out again for another year. In which time, what adventures might have passed her by?

Instead she had returned to work as soon as she felt able, hoping that although she had not taken on all her former responsibilities the familiar routines would help her to re-establish a normal life. But the sleight-of-hand was not entirely successful. Every few days something would happen – she would overhear some remark, or catch a look that she was not intended to see – that made her realise she was being treated with a rehearsed caution; that her colleagues viewed her as being fundamentally changed by her illness. It had made her angry. She'd wanted to spit her suspicions in their faces; tell them that she and her uterus were not synonymous, and that the removal of one did not imply the eclipse of the other.

But today, returning to the office, she was not so certain they weren't correct. She felt as though she hadn't slept in weeks, though in fact she was sleeping long and deeply every night. Her eyesight was blurred, and there was a curious remoteness about her experiences that day that she associated with extreme fatigue, as if she were drifting further and further from the work on her desk; from her sensations, from her very thoughts. Twice that morning she caught herself speaking and then wondered who it was who was conceiving of these words. It certainly wasn't *her*; she was too busy listening.

And then, an hour after lunch, things had suddenly taken a turn for the worse. She had been called into her supervisor's office and asked to sit down.

'Are you all right, Elaine?' Mr Chimes had asked.

'Yes,' she'd told him. 'I'm fine.'

'There's been some concern –'

'About what?'

Chimes looked slightly embarrassed. 'Your behaviour,' he finally said. 'Please don't think I'm prying, Elaine. It's just that if you need some further time to recuperate –'

'There's nothing wrong with me.'

'But your weeping –'

'What?'

'The way you've been crying today. It concerns us.'

'Cry?' she'd said. 'I don't cry.'

The supervisor seemed baffled. 'But you've been crying all day. You're crying now.'

Elaine put a tentative hand to her cheek. And yes; yes, she *was* crying. Her cheek was wet. She'd stood up, shocked at her own conduct.

'I didn't . . . I didn't know,' she said. Though the words sounded preposterous, they were true. She *hadn't* known. Only now, with the fact pointed out, did she taste tears in her throat and sinuses; and with that taste came a memory of when this eccentricity had begun: in front of the television the night before.

'Why don't you take the rest of the day off?'

'Yes.'

'Take the rest of the week if you'd like,' Chimes said. 'You're a valued member of staff, Elaine; I don't have to tell you that. We don't want you coming to any harm.'

This last remark struck home with stinging force. Did they think she was verging on suicide; was that why she was treated with kid gloves? They were only tears she was shedding, for God's sake, and she was so indifferent to them she had not even known they were falling.

'I'll go home,' she said. 'Thank you for your . . . concern.'

The supervisor looked at her with some dismay. 'It must have been a very traumatic experience,' he said.

13

'We all understand; we really do. If you feel you want to talk about it at any time –'

She declined, but thanked him again and left the office.

Face to face with herself in the mirror of the women's toilets she realised just how bad she looked. Her skin was flushed, her eyes swollen. She did what she could to conceal the signs of this painless grief, then picked up her coat and started home. As she reached the underground station she knew that returning to the empty flat would not be a wise idea. She would brood, she would sleep (so much sleep of late, and so perfectly dreamless) but she would not improve her mental condition by either route. It was the bell of Holy Innocents, tolling in the clear afternoon, that reminded her of the smoke and the square and Mr Kavanagh. There, she decided, was a fit place for her to walk. She could enjoy the sunlight, and think. Maybe she would meet her admirer again.

She found her way back to All Saints easily enough, but there was disappointment awaiting her. The demolition site had been cordoned off, the boundary marked by a row of posts – a red fluorescent ribbon looped between them. The site was guarded by no less than four policemen, who were ushering pedestrians towards a detour around the square. The workers and their hammers had been exiled from the shadows of All Saints and now a very different selection of people – suited and academic – occupied the zone beyond the ribbon, some in furrowed conversation, others standing on the muddy ground and staring up quizzically at the derelict church. The south transept and much of the area around it had been curtained off from public view by an arrangement of tarpaulins and black plastic sheeting. Occasionally somebody would emerge from behind this veil and consult with others on the site. All who did so, she noted, were wearing gloves; one or two were also masked. It was as though they were performing some *ad hoc* surgery in the shelter of the screen. A tumour, perhaps, in the bowels of All Saints.

She approached one of the officers. 'What's going on?'

'The foundations are unstable,' he told her. 'Apparently the place could fall down at any moment.'

'Why are they wearing masks?'

'It's just a precaution against the dust.'

She didn't argue, though this explanation struck her as unlikely.

'If you want to get through to Temple Street you'll have to go round the back,' the officer said.

What she really wanted to do was to stand and watch proceedings, but the proximity of the uniformed quartet intimidated her, and she decided to give up and go home. As she began to make her way back to the main road she caught sight of a familiar figure crossing the end of an adjacent street. It was unmistakably Kavanagh. She called after him, though he had already disappeared, and was pleased to see him step back into view and return a nod to her.

'Well, well –' he said as he came down to meet her. 'I didn't expect to see you again so soon.'

'I came to watch the rest of the demolition,' she said.

His face was ruddy with the cold, and his eyes were shining.

'I'm so pleased,' he said. 'Do you want to have some afternoon tea? There's a place just around the corner.'

'I'd like that.'

As they walked she asked him if he knew what was going on at All Saints.

'It's the crypt,' he said, confirming her suspicions.

15

'They opened it?'

'They certainly found a way in. I was here this morning –'

'About your stones?'

'That's right. They were already putting up the tarpaulins then.'

'Some of them were wearing masks.'

'It won't smell very fresh down there. Not after so long.'

Thinking of the curtain of tarpaulin drawn between her and the mystery within she said: 'I wonder what it's like.'

'A wonderland,' Kavanagh replied.

It was an odd response, and she didn't query it, at least not on the spot. But later, when they'd sat and talked together for an hour, and she felt easier with him, she returned to the comment.

'What you said about the crypt . . .'

'Yes?'

'About it being a wonderland.'

'Did I say that?' he replied, somewhat sheepishly. 'What must you think of me?'

'I was just puzzled. Wondered what you meant.'

'I like places where the dead are,' he said. 'I always have. Cemeteries can be very beautiful, don't you think? Mausoleums and tombs; all the fine craftsmanship that goes into those places. Even the dead may sometimes reward closer scrutiny.' He looked at her to see if he had strayed beyond her taste threshold, but seeing that she only looked at him with quiet fascination, continued. 'They can be very beautiful on occasion. It's a sort of a glamour they have. It's a shame it's wasted on morticians and funeral directors.' He made a small mischievous grin. 'I'm sure there's much to be seen in that crypt. Strange sights. Wonderful sights.'

16

'I only ever saw one dead person. My grandmother. I was very young at the time . . .'

'I trust it was a pivotal experience.'

'I don't think so. In fact I scarcely remember it at all. I only remember how everybody cried.'

'Ah.'

He nodded sagely.

'So selfish,' he said. 'Don't you think? Spoiling a farewell with snot and sobs.' Again, he looked at her to gauge the response; again he was satisfied that she would not take offence. 'We cry for ourselves, don't we? Not for the dead. The dead are past caring.'

She made a small, soft: 'Yes,' and then, more loudly: 'My God, yes. That's right. Always for ourselves . . .'

'You see how much the dead can teach, just by lying there, twiddling their thumb-bones?'

She laughed: he joined her in laughter. She had misjudged him on that initial meeting, thinking his face unused to smiles; it was not. But his features, when the laughter died, swiftly regained that eerie quiescence she had first noticed.

When, after a further half hour of his laconic remarks, he told her he had appointments to keep and had to be on his way, she thanked him for his company, and said:

'Nobody's made me laugh so much in weeks. I'm grateful.'

'You *should* laugh,' he told her. 'It suits you.' Then added: 'You have beautiful teeth.'

She thought of this odd remark when he'd gone, as she did of a dozen others he had made through the afternoon. He was undoubtedly one of the most off-beat individuals she'd ever encountered, but he had come into her life – with his eagerness to talk of crypts and the dead and the beauty of her teeth – at just the right moment. He was the perfect distraction from her buried sorrows, making her present aberrations seem minor stuff beside his own. When she started home she was in high spirits. If she had not known herself better she might have thought herself half in love with him.

On the journey back, and later that evening, she thought particularly of the joke he had made about the dead twiddling their thumb-bones, and that thought led inevitably to the mysteries that lay out of sight in the crypt. Her curiosity, once aroused, was not easily silenced; it grew on her steadily that she badly wanted to slip through that cordon of ribbon and see the burial chamber with her own eyes. It was a desire she would never previously have admitted to herself. (How many times had she walked from the site of an accident, telling herself to control the shameful inquisitiveness she felt?) But Kavanagh had legitimised her appetite with his flagrant enthusiasm for things funereal. Now, with the taboo shed, she wanted to go back to All Saints and look Death in its face, then next time she saw Kavanagh she would have some stories to tell of her own. The idea, no sooner budded, came to full flower, and in the middle of the evening she dressed for the street again and headed back towards the square.

She didn't reach All Saints until well after eleven-thirty, but there were still signs of activity at the site. Lights, mounted on stands and on the wall of the church itself, poured illumination on the scene. A trio of technicians, Kavanagh's so-called removal men, stood outside the tarpaulin shelter, their faces drawn with fatigue, their breath clouding the frosty air. She stayed out of sight and watched the scene. She was growing steadily colder, and her scars had begun to ache, but it was apparent that the night's work on the crypt was more or less over. After some brief exchange with the police, the technicians departed. They had extinguished

18

all but one of the floodlights, leaving the site – church, tarpaulin and rimy mud – in grim chiaroscuro.

The two officers who had been left on guard were not over-conscientious in their duties. What idiot, they apparently reasoned, would come grave-robbing at this hour, and in such temperatures? After a few minutes keeping a foot-stamping vigil they withdrew to the relative comfort of the workmen's hut. When they did not re-emerge, Elaine crept out of hiding and moved as cautiously as possible to the ribbon that divided one zone from the other. A radio had been turned on in the hut; its noise (music for lovers from dusk to dawn, the distant voice purred) covered her crackling advance across the frozen earth.

Once beyond the cordon, and into the forbidden territory beyond, she was not so hesitant. She swiftly crossed the hard ground, its wheel-ploughed furrows like concrete, into the lee of the church. The floodlight was dazzling; by it her breath appeared as solid as yesterday's smoke had seemed. Behind her, the music for lovers murmured on. No one emerged from the hut to summon her from her trespassing. No alarm-bells rang. She reached the edge of the tarpaulin curtain without incident, and peered at the scene concealed behind it.

The demolition men, under very specific instructions to judge by the care they had taken in their labours, had dug fully eight feet down the side of All Saints, exposing the foundations. In so doing they had uncovered an entrance to the burial-chamber which previous hands had been at pains to conceal. Not only had earth been piled up against the flank of the church to hide the entrance, but the crypt door had also been removed, and stone masons sealed the entire aperture up. This had clearly been done at some speed; their handiwork was far from ordered. They had simply filled the entrance up with any stone or brick that had come to hand, and plastered coarse mortar over their endeavours. Into this mortar – though the design had been spoiled by the excavations – some artisan had scrawled a six-foot cross.

All their efforts in securing the crypt, and marking the mortar to keep the godless out, had gone for nothing however. The seal had been broken – the mortar hacked at, the stones torn away. There was now a small hole in the middle of the doorway, large enough for one person to gain access to the interior. Elaine had no hesitation in climbing down the slope to the breached wall, and then squirming through.

She had predicted the darkness she met on the other side, and had brought with her a cigarette lighter Mitch had given her three years ago. She flicked it on. The flame was small; she turned up the wick, and by the swelling light investigated the space ahead of her. It was not the crypt itself she had stepped into but a narrow vestibule of some kind: a yard or so in front of her was another wall, and another door. This one had not been replaced with bricks, though into its solid timbers a second cross had been gouged. She approached the door. The lock had been removed – by the investigators presumably – and the door then held shut again with a rope binding. This had been done quickly, by tired fingers. She did not find the rope difficult to untie, though it required both hands, and so had to be effected in the dark.

As she worked the knot free, she heard voices. The policemen – damn them – had left the seclusion of their hut and come out into the bitter night to do their rounds. She let the rope be, and pressed herself against the inside wall of the vestibule. The officers' voices were becoming louder: talking of their children, and the escalating cost of Christmas joy. Now they were within yards of the crypt entrance, standing, or so she guessed, in the shelter of the tarpaulin. They made no attempt to descend the slope however, but finished their cursory inspection on the lip of the earthworks, then turned back. Their voices faded.

Satisfied that they were out of sight and hearing of her, she reignited the flame and returned to the door. It was large and brutally heavy; her first attempt at hauling it open met with little success. She tried again, and this time it moved, grating across the grit on the vestibule floor. Once it was open the vital inches required for her to squeeze through she eased her straining. The lighter guttered as though a breath had blown from within; the flame briefly burned not yellow but electric blue. She didn't pause to admire it, but slid into the promised wonderland.

Now the flame fed – became livid – and for an instant its sudden brightness took her sight away. She pressed the corners of her eyes to clear them, and looked again.

So this was Death. There was none of the art or the glamour Kavanagh had talked of; no calm laying out of shrouded beauties on cool marble sheets; no elaborate reliquaries, nor aphorisms on the nature of human frailty: not even names and dates. In most cases, the corpses lacked even coffins.

The crypt was a charnel-house. Bodies had been thrown in heaps on every side; entire families pressed into niches that were designed to hold a single casket, dozens more left where hasty and careless hands had tossed them. The scene – though absolutely still – was rife with panic. It was there in the faces that stared from the piles of dead: mouths wide in silent protest, sockets in which eyes had withered gaping in shock at

21

such treatment. It was there too in the way the system of burial had degenerated from the ordered arrangement of caskets at the far end of the crypt to the haphazard piling of crudely made coffins, their wood unplaned, their lids unmarked but for a scrawled cross, and thence – finally – to this hurried heaping of unhoused carcasses, all concern for dignity, perhaps even for the rites of passage, forgotten in the rising hysteria.

There had been a disaster, of that she could have no doubt; a sudden influx of bodies – men, women, children (there was a baby at her feet who could not have lived a day) – who had died in such escalating numbers that there was not even time to close their eyelids before they were shunted away into this pit. Perhaps the coffin-makers had also died, and were thrown here amongst their clients; the shroud-sewers too, and the priests. All gone in one apocalyptic month (or week), their surviving relatives too shocked or too frightened to consider the niceties, but only eager to have the dead thrust out of sight where they would never have to look on their flesh again.

There was much of that flesh still in evidence. The sealing of the crypt, closing it off from the decaying air, had kept the occupants intact. Now, with the violation of this secret chamber, the heat of decay had been rekindled, and the tissues were deteriorating afresh. Everywhere she saw rot at work, making sores and suppurations, blisters and pustules. She raised the flame to see better, though the stench of spoilage was beginning to crowd upon her and make her dizzy. Everywhere her eyes travelled she seemed to alight upon some pitiful sight. Two children laid together as if sleeping in each other's arms; a woman whose last act, it appeared, had been to paint her sickened face so as to die more fit for the marriage-bed than the grave.

She could not help but stare, though her fascination cheated them of privacy. There was so much to see and remember. She could never be the same, could she, having viewed these scenes? One corpse – lying half-hidden beneath another – drew her particular attention: a woman whose long chestnut-coloured hair flowed from her scalp so copiously Elaine envied it. She moved closer to get a better look, and then, putting the last of her squeamishness to flight, took hold of the body thrown across the woman, and hauled it away. The flesh of the corpse was greasy to the touch, and left her fingers stained, but she was not distressed. The uncovered corpse lay with her legs wide, but the constant weight of her companion had bent them into an impossible configuration. The wound that had killed her had bloodied her thighs, and glued her skirt to her abdomen and groin. Had she miscarried, Elaine wondered, or had some disease devoured her there?

She stared and stared, bending close to study the faraway look on the woman's rotted face. Such a place to lie, she thought, with your blood still shaming you. She would tell Kavanagh when next she saw him, how wrong he had been with his sentimental tales of calm beneath the sod.

She had seen enough; more than enough. She wiped her hands upon her coat and made her way back to the door, closing it behind her and knotting up the rope again as she had found it. Then she climbed the slope into the clean air. The policemen were nowhere in sight, and she slipped away unseen, like a shadow's shadow.

There was nothing for her to feel, once she had mastered her˜ initial disgust, and that twinge of pity she'd felt seeing the children and the woman with the chestnut hair; and even those responses – even the pity and the repugnance – were quite manageable. She had felt both more acutely seeing a dog run down by a car than she had standing in the crypt of All Saints, despite the horrid displays on every side. When she laid her head down to sleep that night, and realised that she was neither trembling nor nauseous, she felt strong. What was there to fear in all the world if the spectacle of mortality she had just witnessed could be borne so readily? She slept deeply, and woke refreshed.

She went back to work that morning, apologising to Chimes for her behaviour of the previous day, and reassuring him that she was now feeling happier than she'd felt in months. In order to prove her rehabilitation she was as gregarious as she could be, striking up conversations with neglected acquaintances, and giving her smile a ready airing. This met with some initial resistance; she could sense her colleagues doubting that this bout of sunshine actually meant a summer. But when the mood was sustained throughout the day and through the day following, they began to respond more readily. By Thursday it was as though the tears of earlier in the week had never been shed. People told her how well she was looking. It was true; her mirror confirmed the rumours. Her eyes shone, her skin shone. She was a picture of vitality.

On Thursday afternoon she was sitting at her desk, working through a backlog of inquiries, when one of the secretaries appeared from the corridor and began to babble. Somebody went to the woman's aid; through the sobs it was apparent she was talking about Bernice, a woman Elaine knew well enough to exchange smiles with on the stairs, but no better. There had been an accident, it seemed; the woman was talking about blood on the floor. Elaine got up and joined those who were making their way out to see what the fuss was about. The supervisor was already standing outside the women's lavatories, vainly instructing the curious to keep clear. Somebody else – another witness, it seemed – was offering her account of events:

'She was just standing there, and suddenly she started to shake. I thought she was having a fit. Blood started to come from her nose. Then from her mouth. Pouring out.'

'There's nothing to see,' Chimes insisted. 'Please keep back.' But he was substantially ignored. Blankets were being brought to wrap around the woman, and as soon as the toilet door was opened again the sight-seers pressed forward. Elaine caught sight of a form moving about on the toilet floor as if convulsed by cramps; she had no wish to see any more. Leaving the others to throng the corridor, talking loudly of Bernice as if she were already dead, Elaine returned to her desk. She had so much to do; so many wasted, grieving days to catch up on. An apt phrase flitted into her head. *Redeem the time*. She wrote the three words on her notebook as a reminder. Where did they come from? She couldn't recall. It didn't matter. Sometimes there was wisdom in forgetting.

Kavanagh rang her that evening, and invited her out to dinner the following night. She had to decline, however, eager as she was to discuss her recent exploits, because a small party was being thrown by several of her friends, to celebrate her return to health. Would he care to join them? she asked. He thanked her for the invitation, but replied that large numbers of people had always intimidated him. She told him not to be foolish: that her circle would be pleased to meet him, and she to show him off, but he replied he would only put in an appearance if his ego felt the equal of it, and that if he didn't show up he hoped she wouldn't offended.

25

She soothed such fears. Before the conversation came to an end she slyly mentioned that next time they met she had a tale to tell.

The following day brought unhappy news. Bernice had died in the early hours of Friday morning, without ever regaining consciousness. The cause of death was as yet unverified, but the office gossips concurred that she had never been a strong woman – always the first amongst the secretaries to catch a cold and the last to shake it off. There was also some talk, though traded less loudly, about her personal behaviour. She had been generous with her favours it appeared, and injudicious in her choice of partners. With venereal diseases reaching epidemic proportions, was that not the likeliest explanation for the death?

The news, though it kept the rumourmongers in business, was not good for general morale. Two girls went sick that morning, and at lunchtime it seemed that Elaine was the only member of staff with an appetite. She compensated for the lack in her colleagues, however. She had a fierce hunger in her; her body almost seemed to ache for sustenance. It was a good feeling, after so many months of lassitude. When she looked around at the worn faces at the table she felt utterly apart from them: from their tittle-tattle and their trivial opinions, from the way their talk circled on the suddenness of Bernice's death as though they had not given the subject a moment's thought in years, and were amazed that their neglect had not rendered it extinct.

Elaine knew better. She had come close to death so often in the recent past: during the months leading up to her hysterectomy, when the tumours had suddenly doubled in size as though sensing that they were plotted against; on the operating table, when twice the surgeons thought they'd lost her; and most recently, in the crypt, face to face with those gawping carcasses. Death was everywhere. That they should be so startled by its entrance into their charmless circle struck her as almost comical. She ate lustily, and let them talk in whispers.

They gathered for her party at Reuben's house – Elaine, Hermione, Sam and Nellwyn, Josh and Sonja. It was a good night; a chance to pick up on how mutual friends were faring; how statuses and ambitions were on the change. Everyone got drunk very quickly; tongues already loosened by familiarity became progressively looser. Nellwyn led a tearful toast to Elaine; Josh and Sonja had a short but acrimonious exchange on the subject of evangelism; Reuben did his impersonations of fellow barristers. It was like old times, except that memory had yet to improve it. Kavanagh did not put in an appearance, and Elaine was glad of it. Despite her protestations when speaking to him she knew he would have felt out of place in such close-knit company.

About half past midnight, when the room had settled into a number of quiet exchanges, Hermione mentioned the yachtsman. Though she was almost across the room, Elaine heard the sailor's name mentioned quite distinctly. She broke off her conversation with Nellwyn and picked her way through the sprawling limbs to join Hermione and Sam.

'I heard you talking about Maybury,' she said.

'Yes,' said Hermione, 'Sam and I were just saying how strange it all was –'

'I saw him on the news,' Elaine said.

'Sad story, isn't it?' Sam commented. 'The way it happened.'

'Why sad?'

'Him saying that: about Death being on the boat with him –'

27

'– And then dying,' Hermione said.

'Dying?' said Elaine. 'When was this?'

'It was in all the papers.'

'I haven't been concentrating that much,' Elaine replied. 'What happened?'

'He was killed,' Sam said. 'They were taking him to the airport to fly him home, and there was an accident. He was killed just like that.' He snapped his middle finger and thumb. 'Out like a light.'

'So sad,' said Hermione.

She glanced at Elaine, and a frown crept across her face. The look baffled Elaine until – with that same shock of recognition she'd felt in Chimes' office, discovering her tears – she realized that she was smiling.

So the sailor was dead.

When the party broke up in the early hours of Saturday morning – when the embraces and the kisses were over and she was home again – she thought over the Maybury interview she'd heard, summoning a face scorched by the sun and eyes peeled by the wastes he'd almost been lost to, thinking of his mixture of detachment and faint embarrassment as he'd told the tale of his stowaway. And, of course, those final words of his, when pressed to identify the stranger:

'Death, I suppose,' he'd said.

He'd been right.

She woke up late on Saturday morning, without the anticipated hangover. There was a letter from Mitch. She didn't open it, but left it on the mantelpiece for an idle moment later in the day. The first snow of winter was in the wind, though it was too wet to make any serious impression on the streets. The chill was biting enough however, to judge by the scowls on the faces of passers-by. She felt oddly immune from it, however. Though she had no heating on in the flat she walked around in her bathrobe, and barefoot, as though she had a fire stoked in her belly.

After coffee she went through to wash. There was a spider clot of hair in the plug hole; she fished it out and dropped it down the lavatory, then returned to the sink. Since the removal of the dressings she had studiously avoided any close scrutiny of her body, but today her qualms and her vanity seemed to have disappeared. She stripped off her robe, and looked herself over critically.

She was pleased with what she saw. Her breasts were full and dark, her skin had a pleasing sheen to it, her pubic hair had regrown more lushly than ever. The scars themselves still looked and felt tender, but her eyes read their lividness as a sign of her cunt's ambition, as though any day now her sex would grow from anus to navel (and beyond perhaps) opening her up; making her terrible.

It was paradoxical, surely, that it was only now, when the surgeons had emptied her out, that she should feel so ripe, so resplendent. She stood for fully half an hour in front of the mirror admiring herself, her thoughts drifting off. Eventually she returned to the chore of washing. That done, she went back into the front room, still naked. She had no desire to conceal herself; quite the other way about. It was all she could do to prevent herself from stepping out into the snow and giving the whole street something to remember her by.

She crossed to the window, thinking a dozen such foolish thoughts. The snow had thickened. Through the flurries she caught a movement in the alley between the houses opposite. Somebody was there, watching her, though she couldn't see who. She didn't mind. She stood peeping at the peeper, wondering if he would have the courage to show himself, but he did not.

She watched for several minutes before she realised that her brazenness had frightened him away. Disappointed, she wandered back to the bedroom and got dressed. It was time she found herself something to eat; she had that familiar fierce hunger upon her. The fridge was practically empty. She would have to go out and stock up for the weekend.

Supermarkets were circuses, especially on a Saturday, but her mood was far too buoyant to be depressed by having to make her way through the crowds. Today she even found some pleasure in these scenes of conspicuous consumption; in the trolleys and the baskets heaped high with foodstuffs, and the children greedy-eyed as they approached the confectionery, and tearful if denied it, and the wives weighing up the merits of a leg of mutton while their husbands watched the girls on the staff with eyes no less calculating.

She purchased twice as much food for the weekend as she would normally have done in a full week, her appetite driven to distraction by the smells from the delicatessen and fresh meat counters. By the time she reached the house she was almost shaking with the anticipation of sustenance. As she put the bags down on the front step and fumbled for her keys she heard a car door slam behind her.

'Elaine?'

It was Hermione. The red wine she'd consumed the previous night had left her looking blotchy and stale.

'Are you feeling all right?' Elaine asked.

'The point is, are you?' Hermione wanted to know.

'Yes, I'm fine. Why shouldn't I be?'

Hermione returned a harried look. 'Sonja's gone down with some kind of food poisoning, and so's

Reuben. I just came round to see that you were all right.'

'As I say, fine.'

'I don't understand it.'

'What about Nellwyn and Dick?'

'I couldn't get an answer at their place. But Reuben's in a bad way. They've taken him into hospital for tests.'

'Do you want to come in and have a cup of coffee?'

'No thanks, I've got to get back to see Sonja. I just didn't like to think of your being on your own if you'd gone down with it too.'

Elaine smiled. 'You're an angel,' she said, and kissed Hermione on the cheek. The gesture seemed to startle the other woman. For some reason she stepped back, the kiss exchanged, staring at Elaine with a vague puzzlement in her eyes.

'I must . . . I must go,' she said, fixing her face as though it would betray her.

'I'll call you later in the day,' Elaine said, 'and find out how they're doing.'

'Fine.'

Hermione turned away and crossed the pavement to her car. Though she made a cursory attempt to conceal the gesture, Elaine caught sight of her putting her fingers to the spot on her cheek where she had been kissed and scratching at it, as if to eradicate the contact.

It was not the season for flies, but those that had survived the recent cold buzzed around in the kitchen as Elaine selected some bread, smoked ham, and garlic sausage from her purchases, and sat down to eat. She was ravenous. In five minutes or less she had devoured the meats, and made substantial inroads into the loaf, and her hunger was scarcely tamed. Settling to a dessert of figs and cheese, she thought of the paltry omelette she'd been unable to finish that day after the visit to the hospital. One thought led to another; from omelette to smoke to the square to Kavanagh to her most recent visit to the church, and thinking of the place she was suddenly seized by an enthusiasm to see it one final time before it was entirely levelled. She was probably too late already. The bodies would have been parcelled up and removed, the crypt decontaminated and scoured; the walls would be rubble. But she knew she would not be satisfied until she had seen it for herself.

Even after a meal which would have sickened her with its excess a few days before, she felt light-headed as she set out for All Saints; almost as though she were drunk. Not the maudlin drunkenness she had been prone to when with Mitch, but a euphoria which made her feel well-nigh invulnerable, as if she had at last located some bright and incorruptible part of herself, and no harm would ever befall her again.

She had prepared herself for finding All Saints in ruins, but she did not. The building still stood, its walls untouched, its beams still dividing the sky. Perhaps it too could not be toppled, she mused; perhaps she and it were twin immortals. The suspicion was reinforced by the gaggle of fresh worshippers the church had attracted. The police guard had trebled since the day she'd been here, and the tarpaulin that had shielded the crypt entrance from sight was now a vast tent, supported by scaffolding, which entirely encompassed the flank of the building. The altar-servers, standing in close proximity to the tent, wore masks and gloves; the high priests – the chosen few who were actually allowed into the Holy of Holies – were entirely garbed in protective suits.

She watched from the cordon: the signs and genuflections between the devotees; the sluicing down of the suited men as they emerged from behind the veil; the fine spray of fumigants which filled the air like bitter incense.

Another onlooker was quizzing one of the officers.

'Why the suits?'

'In case it's contagious,' the reply came.

'After all these years?'

'They don't know what they've got in there.'

'Diseases don't last, do they?'

'It's a plague-pit,' the officer said. 'They're just being cautious.'

Elaine listened to the exchange, and her tongue itched to speak. She could save them their investigations with a few words. After all, she was living proof that whatever pestilence had destroyed the families in the crypt it was no longer virulent. She had breathed that air, she had touched that mouldy flesh, and she felt healthier now than she had in years. But they would not thank her for her revelations, would they? They were too engrossed in their rituals; perhaps even excited by the discovery of such horrors, their turmoil fuelled and fired by the possibility that this death was still living. She would not be so unsporting as to sour their enthusiasm with a confession of her own rare good health.

Instead she turned her back on the priests and their rites, on the drizzle of incense in the air, and began to walk away from the square. As she looked up from her thoughts she glimpsed a familiar figure watching her from the corner of the adjacent street. He turned away as she glanced up, but it was undoubtedly Kavanagh. She called to him, and went to the corner, but he was walking smartly away from her, head bowed. Again she called after him, and now he turned – a patently false look of surprise pasted onto his face – and retrod his escape-route to greet her.

'Have you heard what they've found?' she asked him.

'Oh yes,' he replied. Despite the familiarity they'd last enjoyed she was reminded now of her first impression of him: that he was not a man much conversant with feeling.

'Now you'll never get your stones,' she said.

'I suppose not,' he replied, not overtly concerned at the loss.

She wanted to tell him that she'd seen the plague-pit with her own eyes, hoping the news would bring a gleam to his face, but the corner of this sunlit street was an inappropriate spot for such talk. Besides, it was almost as if he knew. He looked at her so oddly, the warmth of their previous meeting entirely gone.

'Why did you come back?' he asked her.

'Just to see,' she replied.

'I'm flattered.'

'Flattered?'

'That my enthusiasm for mausoleums is infectious.'

Still he watched her, and she, returning his look, was conscious of how cold his eyes were, and how perfectly shiny. They might have been glass, she thought; and his skin suede-glued like a hood over the subtle architecture of his skull.

'I should go,' she said.

'Business or pleasure?'

'Neither,' she told him. 'One or two of my friends are ill.'

'Ah.'

She had the impression that he wanted to be away; that it was only fear of foolishness that kept him from running from her.

'Perhaps I'll see you again,' she said. 'Sometime.'

'I'm sure,' he replied, gratefully taking his cue and retreating along the street. 'And to your friends – my best regards.'

Even if she wanted to pass Kavanagh's good wishes along to Reuben and Sonja, she could not have done so. Hermione did not answer the telephone, nor did any of the others. The closest she came was to leave a message with Reuben's answering service.

The light-headedness she'd felt earlier in the day developed into a strange dreaminess as the afternoon inched towards evening. She ate again, but the feast did nothing to keep the fugue-state from deepening. She felt quite well; that sense of inviolability that had came upon her was still intact. But time and again as the day wore on she found herself standing on the threshold of a room not knowing why she had come there; or watching the light dwindle in the street outside without being quite certain if she was the viewer or the thing viewed. She was happy with her company though, as the flies were happy. They kept buzzing attendance even though the dark fell.

About seven in the evening she heard a car draw up outside, and the bell rang. She went to the door of her flat, but couldn't muster the inquisitiveness to open it, step out into the hallway and admit callers. It would be Hermione again, most probably, and she didn't have any appetite for gloomy talk. Didn't want anybody's company in fact, but that of the flies.

The callers insisted on the bell; the more they insisted the more determined she became not to reply. She slid down the wall beside the flat door and listened to the muted debate that now began on the step. It wasn't Hermione; it was nobody she recognized. Now they systematically rang the bells of the flats above, until

Mr Prudhoe came down from the top flat, talking to himself as he went, and opened the door to them. Of the conversation that followed she caught sufficient only to grasp the urgency of their mission, but her dishevelled mind hadn't the persistence to attend to the details. They persuaded Prudhoe to allow them into the hallway. They approached the door of her flat and rapped upon it, calling her name. She didn't reply. They rapped again, exchanging words of frustration. She wondered if they could hear her smiling in the darkness. At last – after a further exchange with Prudhoe – they left her to herself.

She didn't know how long she sat on her haunches beside the door, but when she stood up again her lower limbs were entirely numb, and she was hungry. She ate voraciously, more or less finishing off all the purchases of that morning. The flies seemed to have procreated in the intervening hours; they crawled on the table and picked at her slops. She let them eat. They too had their lives to live.

Finally she decided to take some air. No sooner had she stepped out of her flat, however, than the vigilant Prudhoe was at the top of the stairs, and calling down to her.

'Miss Rider. Wait a moment. I have a message for you.'

She contemplated closing the door on him, but she knew he would not rest until he had delivered his communiqué. He hurried down the stairs – a Cassandra in shabby slippers.

'There were policemen here,' he announced before he had even reached the bottom step, 'they were looking for you.'

'Oh,' she said. 'Did they say what they wanted?'

'To talk to you. *Urgently*. Two of your friends –'

'What about them?'

'They died,' he said. 'This afternoon. They have some kind of disease.'

He had a sheet of notepaper in his hand. This he now passed over to her, relinquishing his hold an instant before she took it.

'They left that number for you to call,' he said. 'You've to contact them as soon as possible.' His message delivered, he was already retiring up the stairs again.

Elaine looked down at the sheet of paper, with its scrawled figures. By the time she'd read the seven digits, Prudhoe had disappeared.

She went back into the flat. For some reason she wasn't thinking of Reuben or Sonja – who, it seemed, she would not see again – but of the sailor, Maybury, who'd seen Death and escaped it only to have it follow him like a loyal dog, waiting its moment to leap and lick his face. She sat beside the phone and stared at the numbers on the sheet, and then at the fingers that held the sheet and at the hands that held the fingers. Was the touch that hung so innocently at the end of her arms now lethal? Was that what the detectives had come to tell her? That her friends were dead by *her* good offices? If so, how many others had she brushed against and breathed upon in the days since her pestilential education at the crypt? In the street, in the bus, in the supermarket: at work, at play. She thought of Bernice, lying on the toilet floor, and of Hermione, rubbing the spot where she had been kissed as if knowing some scourge had been passed along to her. And suddenly she *knew*, knew in her marrow, that her pursuers were right in their suspicions, and that all these dreamy days she had been nurturing a fatal child. Hence her hunger; hence the glow of fulfilment she felt.

She put down the note and sat in the semi-darkness, trying to work out precisely the plague's location. Was it her fingertips; in her belly; in her eyes? None, and yet all of these. Her first assumption had been wrong. It wasn't a child at all: she didn't carry it in some particular cell. It was *everywhere*. She and it were synonymous. That being so, there could be no slicing out of the offending part, as they had sliced out her tumours and all that had been devoured by them. Not that she would escape their attentions for that fact. They had come looking for her, hadn't they, to take her back into the custody of sterile rooms, to deprive her of her opinions and dignity, to make her fit only for their loveless investigations. The thought revolted her; she would rather die as the chestnut-haired woman in the crypt had died, sprawled in agonies, than submit to them again. She tore up the sheet of paper and let the litter drop.

It was too late for solutions anyway. The removal men had opened the door and found Death waiting on the other side, eager for daylight. She was its agent, and it – in its wisdom – had granted her immunity; had given her strength and a dreamy rapture; had taken her fear away. She, in return, had spread its word, and there was no undoing those labours: not now. All the dozens, maybe hundreds, of people whom she'd contaminated in the last few days would have gone back to their families and friends, to their work places and their places of recreation, and spread the word yet further. They would have passed its fatal promise to their children as they tucked them into bed, and to their mates in the act of love. Priests had no doubt given it with Communion; shopkeepers with change of a five-pound note.

While she was thinking of this – of the disease spreading like fire in tinder – the doorbell rang again. They had come back for her. And, as before, they

38

were ringing the other bells in the house. She could hear Prudhoe coming downstairs. This time he would know she was in. He would tell them so. They would hammer at the door, and when she refused to answer –

As Prudhoe opened the front door she unlocked the back. As she slipped into the yard she heard voices at the flat door, and then their rapping and their demands. She unbolted the yard gate and fled into the darkness of the alley-way. She already out of hearing range by the time they had beaten down the door.

She wanted most of all to go back to All Saints, but she knew that such a tactic would only invite arrest. They would expect her to follow that route, counting upon her adherence to the first cause. But she wanted to see Death's face again, now more than ever. To speak with it. To debate its strategies. *Their* strategies. To ask why it had chosen her.

She emerged from the alley-way and watched the goings-on at the front of the house from the corner of the street. This time there were more than two men; she counted four at least, moving in and out of the house. What were they doing? Peeking through her underwear and her love-letters, most probably, examining the sheets on her bed for stray hairs, and the mirror for traces of her reflection. But even if they turned the flat upside-down, if they examined every print and pronoun, they wouldn't find the clues they sought. Let them search. The lover had escaped. Only her tear stains remained, and flies at the light bulb to sing her praises.

The night was starry, but as she walked down to the centre of the city the brightness of the Christmas illuminations festooning trees and buildings cancelled out their light. Most of the stores were well closed by this hour, but a good number of window-shoppers still idled along the pavements. She soon tired of the displays however, of the baubles and the dummies, and made her way off the main road and into the side streets. It was darker here, which suited her abstracted state of mind. The sound of music and laughter escaped through open bar doors; an argument erupted in an upstairs gaming-room: blows were exchanged; in one doorway two lovers defied discretion; in another, a man pissed with the gusto of a horse.

It was only now, in the relative hush of these backwaters, that she realised she was not alone. Footsteps followed her, keeping a cautious distance, but never straying far. Had the trackers followed her? Were they hemming her in even now, preparing to snatch her into their closed order? If so, flight would only delay the inevitable. Better to confront them now, and dare them to come within range of her pollution. She slid into hiding, and listened as the footsteps approached, then stepped into view.

It was not the law, but Kavanagh. Her initial shock was almost immediately superseded by a sudden comprehension of *why* he had pursued her. She studied him. His skin was pulled so tight over his skull she could see the bone gleam in the dismal light. How, her whirling thoughts demanded, had she not recognised him sooner? Not realised at that first meeting, when he'd talked of the dead and their glamour, that he spoke as their Maker?

'I followed you,' he said.

'All the way from the house?'

He nodded.

'What did they tell you?' he asked her. 'The policemen. What did they say?'

40

'Nothing I hadn't already guessed,' she replied.

'You knew?'

'In a manner of speaking. I must have done, in my heart of hearts. Remember our first conversation?'

He murmured that he did.

'All you said about Death. Such egotism.'

He grinned suddenly, showing more bone.

'Yes,' he said. 'What must you think of me?'

'It made a kind of sense to me, even then. I didn't know why at the time. Didn't know what the future would bring –'

'What does it bring?' he inquired of her softly.

She shrugged. 'Death's been waiting for me all this time, am I right?'

'Oh yes,' he said, pleased by her understanding of the situation between them. He took a step towards her, and reached to touch her face.

'You are remarkable,' he said.

'Not really.'

'But to be so unmoved by it all. So cold.'

'What's to be afraid of?' she said. He stroked her cheek. She almost expected his hood of skin to come unbuttoned then, and the marbles that played in his sockets to tumble out and smash. But he kept his disguise intact, for appearance's sake.

'I want you,' he told her.

'Yes,' she said. Of course he did. It had been in his every word from the beginning, but she hadn't had the wit to comprehend it. Every love story was – at the last – a story of death; this was what the poets insisted. Why should it be any less true the other way about?

They could not go back to his house; the officers would be there too, he told her, for they must know of the romance between them. Nor, of course, could they return to her flat. So they found a small hotel in the vicinity and took a room there. Even in the dingy lift he took the liberty of stroking her hair, and then, finding her compliant, put his hand upon her breast.

The room was sparsely furnished, but was lent some measure of charm by a splash of coloured lights from a Christmas tree in the street below. Her lover didn't take his eyes off her for a single moment, as if even now he expected her to turn tail and run at the merest flaw in his behaviour. He needn't have concerned himself; his treatment of her left little cause for complaint. His kisses were insistent but not overpowering; his undressing of her – except for the fumbling (a nice human touch, she thought) – was a model of finesse and sweet solemnity.

She was surprised that he had not known about her scar, only because she had become to believe this intimacy had begun on the operating table, when twice she had gone into his arms, and twice been denied them by the surgeon's bullying. But perhaps, being no sentimentalist, he had forgotten that first meeting. Whatever the reason, he looked to be upset when he slipped off her dress, and there was a trembling interval when she thought he would reject her. But the moment passed, and now he reached down to her abdomen and ran his fingers along the scar.

'It's beautiful,' he said.

She was happy.

'I almost died under the anaesthetic,' she told him.

'That would have been a waste,' he said, reaching up her body and working at her breast. It seemed to arouse him, for his voice was more guttural when next he spoke. 'What did they tell you?' he asked her, moving his hands up the soft channel behind her clavicle, and stroking her there. She had not been touched in months, except by disinfected hands; his delicacy woke shivers in her. She was so engrossed in pleasure that she failed to reply to his question. He asked again as he moved between her legs.

'What did they tell you?'

Through a haze of anticipation she said: 'They left a number for me to ring. So that I could be helped . . .'

'But you didn't want help?'

'No,' she breathed. 'Why should I?'

She half-saw his smile, though her eyes wanted to flicker closed entirely. His appearance failed to stir any passion in her; indeed there was much about his disguise (that absurd bow-tie, for one) which she thought ridiculous. With her eyes closed, however, she could forget such petty details; she could strip the hood off and imagine him pure. When she thought of him that way her mind pirouetted.

He took his hands from her; she opened her eyes. He was fumbling with his belt. As he did so somebody shouted in the street outside. His head jerked in the direction of the window; his body tensed. She was surprised at his sudden concern.

'It's all right,' she said.

He leaned forward and put his hand to her throat.

'Be quiet,' he instructed.

She looked up into his face. He had begun to sweat. The exchanges in the street went on for a few minutes longer; it was simply two late-night gamblers parting. He realized his error now.

'I thought I heard -'

'What?'

'- I thought I heard them calling my name.'

'Who would do that?' she inquired fondly. 'Nobody knows we're here.'

He looked away from the window. All purposefulness had abruptly drained from him; after the instant of fear his features had slackened. He looked almost stupid.

'They came close,' he said. 'But they never found me.'

'Close?'

'Coming to you.' He laid his head on her breasts. 'So *very* close,' he murmured. She could hear her pulse in her head. 'But I'm swift,' he said, 'and invisible.'

His hand strayed back down to her scar, and further.

'And always neat,' he added.

She sighed as he stroked her.

'They admire me for that, I'm sure. Don't you think they must admire me? For being so neat?'

She remembered the chaos of the crypt; its indignities, its disorders.

'Not always . . .' she said.

He stopped stroking her.

'*Oh yes*,' he said. 'Oh yes. I never spill blood. That's a rule of mine. *Never* spill blood.'

She smiled at his boasts. She would tell him now – though surely he already knew – about her visit to All Saints, and the handiwork of his that she'd seen there.

'Sometimes you can't help blood being spilt,' she said, 'I don't hold it against you.'

At these words, he began to tremble.

'What did they tell you about me? What *lies*?'

'Nothing,' she said, mystified by his response. 'What could they know?'

'I'm a professional,' he said to her, his hand moving back up to her face. She felt intentionality in him again. A seriousness in his weight as he pressed closer upon her.

'I won't have them lie about me,' he said. 'I won't have it.'

He lifted his head from her chest and looked at her.

'All I do is stop the drummer,' he said.

'The drummer?'

'I have to stop him cleanly. In his tracks.'

The wash of colours from the lights below painted his face one moment red, the next green, the next yellow; unadulterated hues, as in a child's paint-box.

'I won't have them tell lies about me,' he said again. 'To say I spill blood.'

'They told me nothing,' she assured him. He had given up his pillow entirely, and now moved to straddle her. His hands were done with tender touches.

'Shall I show you how clean I am?' he said: 'How easily I stop the drummer?'

Before she could reply, his hands closed around her neck. She had no time even to gasp, let alone shout. His thumbs were expert; they found her windpipe and pressed. She heard the drummer quicken its rhythm in her ears. 'It's quick; and clean,' he was telling her, the colours still coming in predictable sequence. Red, yellow, green; red, yellow, green.

There was an error here, she knew; a terrible misunderstanding which she couldn't quite fathom. She struggled to make some sense of it.

'I don't understand,' she tried to tell him, but her bruised larynx could produce no more than a gargling sound.

'Too late for excuses,' he said, shaking his head. 'You came to me, remember? You want the drummer stopped. Why else did you come?' His grip tightened yet further. She had the sensation of her face swelling; of the blood throbbing to jump from her eyes.

'Don't you see that they came to warn you about me?' frowning as he laboured. 'They came to seduce you away from me by telling you I spilt blood.'

'*No*,' she squeezed the syllable out on her last breath, but he only pressed harder to cancel her denial.

45

The drummer was deafeningly loud now; though Kavanagh's mouth still opened and closed she could no longer hear what he was telling her. It mattered little. She realised now that he was not Death; not the clean-boned guardian she'd waited for. In her eagerness, she had given herself into the hands of a common killer, a street-corner Cain. She wanted to spit contempt at him, but her consciousness was slipping, the room, the lights, the face all throbbing to the drummer's beat. And then it all stopped.

She looked down on the bed. Her body lay sprawled across it. One desperate hand had clutched at the sheet, and clutched still, though there was no life left in it. Her tongue protruded, there was spittle on her blue lips. But (as he had promised) there was no blood.

She hovered, her presence failing even to bring a breeze to the cobwebs in this corner of the ceiling, and watched while Kavanagh observed the rituals of his crime. He was bending over the body, whispering in its ear as he rearranged it on the tangled sheets. Then he unbuttoned himself and unveiled that bone whose inflammation was the sincerest form of flattery. What followed was comical in its gracelessness; as her body was comical, with its scars and its places where age puckered and plucked at it. She watched his ungainly attempts at congress quite remotely. His buttocks were pale, and imprinted with the marks his underwear had left; their motion put her in mind of a mechanical toy.

He kissed her as he worked, and swallowed the pestilence with her spittle; his hands came off her body gritty with her contagious cells. He knew none of this, of course. He was perfectly innocent of what corruption he embraced, and took into himself with every uninspired thrust.

46

At last, he finished. There was no gasp, no cry. He simply stopped his clockwork motion and climbed off her, wiping himself with the edge of the sheet, and buttoning himself up again.

Guides were calling her. She had journeys to make, reunions to look forward to. But she did not want to go; at least not yet. She steered the vehicle of her spirit to a fresh vantage-point, where she could better see Kavanagh's face. Her sight, or whatever sense this condition granted her, saw clearly how his features were painted over a groundwork of muscle, and how, beneath that intricate scheme, the bones sheened. Ah, the bone. He was not Death of course; and yet he was. He had the face, hadn't he? And one day, given decay's blessing, he'd show it. Such a pity that a scraping of flesh came between it and the naked eye.

Come away, the voices insisted. She knew they could not be fobbed off very much longer. Indeed there were some amongst them she thought she knew. *A moment*, she pleaded, *only a moment more*.

Kavanagh had finished his business at the murder-scene. He checked his appearance in the wardrobe mirror, then went to the door. She went with him, intrigued by the utter banality of his expression. He slipped out onto the silent landing and then down the stairs, waiting for a moment when the night-porter was otherwise engaged before stepping out into the street, and liberty.

Was it dawn that washed the sky, or the illuminations? Perhaps she had watched him from the corner of the room longer than she'd thought – hours passing as moments in the state she had so recently achieved.

Only at the last was she rewarded for her vigil, as a look she recognised crossed Kavanagh's face. Hunger! The man was hungry. He would not die of the plague, any more than she had. Its presence shone in him – gave a fresh lustre to his skin, and a new insistence to his belly.

He had come to her a minor murderer, and was going from her as Death writ large. She laughed, seeing the self-fulfilling prophecy she had unwittingly engineered. For an instant his pace slowed, as if he might have heard her. But no; it was the drummer he was listening for, beating louder than ever in his ear and demanding, as he went, a new and deadly vigour in his every step.

HOW SPOILERS BLEED

L OCKE RAISED HIS eyes to the trees. The wind was moving in them, and the commotion of their laden branches sounded like the river in full spate. One impersonation of many. When he had first come to the jungle he had been awed by the sheer multiplicity of beast and blossom, the relentless parade of life here. But he had learned better. This burgeoning diversity was a sham; the jungle pretending itself an artless garden. It was not. Where the untutored trespasser saw only a brilliant show of natural splendours, Locke now recognised a subtle conspiracy at work, in which each thing mirrored some other thing. The trees, the river; a blossom, a bird. In a moth's wing, a monkey's eye; on a lizard's back, sunlight on stones. Round and round in a dizzying circle of impersonations, a hall of mirrors which confounded the senses and would, given time, rot reason altogether. See us now, he thought drunkenly as they stood around Cherrick's grave, look at how we play the game too. We're living; but we impersonate the dead better than the dead themselves.

The corpse had been one scab by the time they'd hoisted it into a sack and carried it outside to this miserable plot behind Tetelman's house to bury. There were half a dozen other graves here. All Europeans, to judge by the names crudely burned into the wooden crosses; killed by snakes, or heat, or longing.

Tetelman attempted to say a brief prayer in Spanish, but the roar of the trees, and the din of birds making their way home to their roosts before night came down, all but drowned him out. He gave up eventually, and they made their way back into the cooler interior of the house, where Stumpf was sitting, drinking brandy and staring inanely at the darkening stain on the floorboards.

Outside, two of Tetelman's tamed Indians were shovelling the rank jungle earth on top of Cherrick's sack, eager to be done with the work and away before nightfall. Locke watched from the window. The grave-diggers didn't talk as they laboured, but filled the shallow grave up, then flattened the earth as best they could with the leather-tough soles of their feet. As they did so the stamping of the ground took on a rhythm. It occurred to Locke that the men were probably the worse for bad whisky; he knew few Indians who didn't drink like fishes. Now, staggering a little, they began to dance on Cherrick's grave.

'Locke?'

Locke woke. In the darkness, a cigarette glowed. As the smoker drew on it, and the tip burned more intensely, Stumpf's wasted features swam up out of the night.

'Locke? Are you awake?'

'What do you want?'

'I can't sleep,' the mask replied, 'I've been thinking. The supply plane comes in from Santarem the day after tomorrow. We could be back there in a few hours. Out of all this.'

'Sure.'

'I mean permanently,' Stumpf said. 'Away.'

'Permanently?'

Stumpf lit another cigarette from the embers of his last before saying, 'I don't believe in curses. Don't think I do.'

'Who said anything about curses?'

'You saw Cherrick's body. What happened to him . . .'

'There's a disease,' said Locke, 'what's it called? – when the blood doesn't set properly?'

'Haemophilia,' Stumpf replied. 'He didn't have haemophilia and we both know it. I've seen him scratched and cut dozens of times. He mended like you or I.'

Locke snatched at a mosquito that had alighted on his chest and ground it out between thumb and forefinger.

'All right. Then what killed him?'

'You saw the wounds better than I did, but it seemed to me his skin just broke open as soon as he was touched.'

Locke nodded. 'That's the way it looked.'

'Maybe it's something he caught off the Indians.'

Locke took the point. '*I* didn't touch any of them,' he said.

'Neither did I. But he did, remember?'

Locke remembered; scenes like that weren't easy to forget, try as he might. 'Christ,' he said, his voice hushed. 'What a fucking situation.'

'I'm going back to Santarem. I don't want them coming looking for me.'

51

'They're not going to.'

'How do you know? We screwed up back there. We could have bribed them. Got them off the land some other way.'

'I doubt it. You heard what Tetelman said. Ancestral territories.'

'You can have my share of the land,' Stumpf said, 'I want no part of it.'

'You mean it then? You're getting out?'

'I feel dirty. We're spoilers, Locke.'

'It's your funeral.'

'I mean it. I'm not like you. Never really had the stomach for this kind of thing. Will you buy my third off me?'

'Depends on your price.'

'Whatever you want to give. It's yours.'

Confessional over, Stumpf returned to his bed, and lay down in the darkness to finish off his cigarette. It would soon be light. Another jungle dawn: a precious interval, all too short, before the world began to sweat. How he *hated* the place. At least he hadn't touched any of the Indians; hadn't even been within breathing distance of them. Whatever infection they'd passed on to Cherrick he could surely not be tainted. In less than forty-eight hours he would be away to Santarem, and then on to some city, *any* city, where the tribe could never follow. He'd already done his penance, hadn't he? Paid for his greed and his arrogance with the rot in his abdomen and the terrors he knew he would never quite shake off again. Let that be punishment enough, he prayed, and slipped, before the monkeys began to call up the day, into a spoiler's sleep.

A gem-backed beetle, trapped beneath Stumpf's

mosquito net, hummed around in diminishing circles, looking for some way out. It could find none. Eventually, exhausted by the search, it hovered over the sleeping man, then landed on his forehead. There it wandered, drinking at the pores. Beneath its imperceptible tread, Stumpf's skin opened and broke into a trail of tiny wounds.

They had come into the Indian hamlet at noon; the sun a basilisk's eye. At first they had thought the place deserted. Locke and Cherrick had advanced into the compound, leaving the dysentery-ridden Stumpf in the jeep, out of the worst of the heat. It was Cherrick who first noticed the child. A pot-bellied boy of perhaps four or five, his face painted with thick bands of the scarlet vegetable dye *urucu*, had slipped out from his hiding place and come to peer at the trespassers, fearless in his curiosity. Cherrick stood still; Locke did the same. One by one, from the huts and from the shelter of the trees around the compound, the tribe appeared and stared, like the boy, at the newcomers. If there was a flicker of feeling on their broad, flat-nosed faces, Locke could not read it. These people – he thought of every Indian as part of one wretched tribe – were impossible to decipher; deceit was their only skill.

'What are you doing here?' he said. The sun was baking the back of his neck. 'This is our land.'

The boy still looked up at him. His almond eyes refused to fear.

'They don't understand you,' Cherrick said.

'Get the Kraut out here. Let him explain it to them.'

'He can't move.'

'*Get him out here*,' Locke said. 'I don't care if he's shat his pants.'

53

Cherrick backed away down the track, leaving Locke standing in the ring of huts. He looked from doorway to doorway, from tree to tree, trying to estimate the numbers. There were at most three dozen Indians, two-thirds of them women and children; descendants of the great peoples that had once roamed the Amazon Basin in their tens of thousands. Now those tribes were all but decimated. The forest in which they had prospered for generations was being levelled and burned; eight-lane highways were speeding through their hunting grounds. All they held sacred – the wilderness and their place in its system – was being trampled and trespassed: they were exiles in their own land. But still they declined to pay homage to their new masters, despite the rifles they brought. Only death would convince them of defeat, Locke mused.

Cherrick found Stumpf slumped in the front seat of the jeep, his pasty features more wretched than ever.

'Locke wants you,' he said, shaking the German out of his doze. 'The village is still occupied. You'll have to speak to them.'

Stumpf groaned. 'I can't move,' he said, 'I'm dying –'

'Locke wants you dead or alive,' Cherrick said. Their fear of Locke, which went unspoken, was perhaps one of the two things they had in common; that and greed.

'I feel awful,' Stumpf said.

'If I don't bring you, he'll only come himself,' Cherrick pointed out. This was indisputable. Stumpf threw the other man a despairing glance, then nodded his jowly head. 'All right,' he said, 'help me.'

Cherrick had no wish to lay a hand on Stumpf. The man stank of his sickness; he seemed to be oozing the contents of his gut through his pores; his skin had the lustre of rank meat. He took the outstretched hand nevertheless. Without aid, Stumpf

54

would never make the hundred yards from jeep to compound.

Ahead, Locke was shouting.

'Get moving,' said Cherrick, hauling Stumpf down from the front seat and towards the bawling voice. 'Let's get it over and done with.'

When the two men returned into the circle of huts the scene had scarcely changed. Locke glanced around at Stumpf.

'We got trespassers,' he said.

'So I see,' Stumpf returned wearily.

'Tell them to get the fuck off our land,' Locke said. 'Tell them this is our territory: we bought it. Without sitting tenants.'

Stumpf nodded, not meeting Locke's rabid eyes. Sometimes he hated the man almost as much as he hated himself.

'Go on . . .' Locke said, and gestured for Cherrick to relinquish his support of Stumpf. This he did. The German stumbled forward, head bowed. He took several seconds to work out his patter, then raised his head and spoke a few wilting words in bad Portuguese. The pronouncement was met with the same blank looks as Locke's performance. Stumpf tried again, re-arranging his inadequate vocabulary to try and awake a flicker of understanding amongst these savages.

The boy who had been so entertained by Locke's cavortings now stood staring up at this third demon, his face wiped of smiles. This one was nowhere near as comical as the first. He was sick and haggard; he smelt of death. The boy held his nose to keep from inhaling the badness off the man.

Stumpf peered through greasy eyes at his audience. If they *did* understand, and were faking their blank incomprehension, it was a flawless performance. His limited skills defeated, he turned giddily to Locke.

'They don't understand me,' he said.

'Tell them again.'

'I don't think they speak Portuguese.'

'Tell them anyway.'

Cherrick cocked his rifle. 'We don't have to talk with them,' he said under his breath. 'They're on our land. We're within our rights –'

'No,' said Locke. 'There's no need for shooting. Not if we can persuade them to go peacefully.'

'They don't understand plain common sense,' Cherrick said. 'Look at them. They're animals. Living in filth.'

Stumpf had begun to try and communicate again, this time accompanying his hesitant words with a pitiful mime.

'Tell them we've got work to do here,' Locke prompted him.

'I'm trying my best,' Stumpf replied testily.

'We've got papers.'

'I don't think they'd be much impressed,' Stumpf returned, with a cautious sarcasm that was lost on the other man.

'Just tell them to move on. Find some other piece of land to squat on.'

Watching Stumpf put these sentiments into word and sign-language, Locke was already running through the alternative options available. Either the Indians – the Txukahamei or the Achual or whatever damn family it was – accepted their demands and moved on, or else they would have to enforce the edict. As Cherrick had said, they were within their rights. They had papers from the development authorities; they had maps marking the division between one territory and the next; they

56

had every sanction from signature to bullet. He had no active desire to shed blood. The world was still too full of bleeding heart liberals and doe-eyed sentimentalists to make genocide the most convenient solution. But the gun had been used before, and would be used again, until every unwashed Indian had put on a pair of trousers and given up eating monkeys.

Indeed, the din of liberals notwithstanding, the gun had its appeal. It was swift, and absolute. Once it had had its short, sharp say there was no danger of further debate; no chance that in ten years' time some mercenary Indian who'd found a copy of Marx in the gutter could come back claiming his tribal lands – oil, minerals and all. Once gone, they were gone forever.

At the thought of these scarlet-faced savages laid low, Locke felt his trigger-finger itch; physically *itch*. Stumpf had finished his encore; it had met with no response. Now he groaned, and turned to Locke.

'I'm going to be sick,' he said. His face was bright white; the glamour of his skin made his small teeth look dingy.

'Be my guest,' Locke replied.

'*Please*. I have to lie down. I don't want them watching me.'

Locke shook his head. 'You don't move 'til they listen. If we don't get any joy from them, you're going to see something to be sick about.' Locke toyed with the stock of his rifle as he spoke, running a broken thumb-nail along the nicks in it. There were perhaps a dozen; each one a human grave. The jungle concealed murder so easily; it almost seemed, in its cryptic fashion, to condone the crime.

Stumpf turned away from Locke and scanned the mute assembly. There were so many Indians here, he thought, and though he carried a pistol he was an inept

57

marksman. Suppose they rushed Locke, Cherrick and himself? He would not survive. And yet, looking at the Indians, he could see no sign of aggression amongst them. Once they had been warriors; now? Like beaten children, sullen and wilfully stupid. There was some trace of beauty in one or two of the younger women; their skins, though grimy, were fine, their eyes black. Had he felt more healthy he might have been aroused by their nakedness, tempted to press his hands upon their shiny bodies. As it was their feigned incomprehension merely irritated him. They seemed, in their silence, like another species, as mysterious and unfathomable as mules or birds. Hadn't somebody in Uxituba told him that many of these people didn't even give their children proper names? That each was like a limb of the tribe, anonymous and therefore unfixable? He could believe that now, meeting the same dark stare in each pair of eyes; could believe that what they faced here was not three dozen individuals but a fluid system of hatred made flesh. It made him shudder to think of it.

Now, for the first time since their appearance, one of the assembly moved. He was an ancient; fully thirty years older than most of the tribe. He, like the rest, was all but naked. The sagging flesh of his limbs and breasts resembled tanned hide; his step, though the pale eyes suggested blindness, was perfectly confident. Once standing in front of the interlopers he opened his mouth – there were no teeth set in his rotted gums – and spoke. What emerged from his scraggy throat was not a language made of words, but only of sound; a pot-pourri of jungle noises. There was no discernible pattern to the outpouring, it was simply a display – awesome in its way – of impersonations. The man could murmur like a jaguar, screech like a parrot; he could find in his throat the splash of rain on orchids; the howl of monkeys.

The sounds made Stumpf's gorge rise. The jungle had diseased him, dehydrated him and left him wrung out. Now this rheumy-eyed stick-man was vomiting the whole odious place up at him. The raw heat in the circle of huts made Stumpf's head beat, and he was sure, as he stood listening to the sage's din, that the old man was measuring the rhythm of his nonsense to the thud at his temples and wrists.

'What's he saying?' Locke demanded.

'What does it sound like?' Stumpf replied, irritated by Locke's idiot questions. 'It's all noises.'

'The fucker's cursing us,' Cherrick said.

Stumpf looked round at the third man. Cherrick's eyes were starting from his head.

'It's a curse,' he said to Stumpf.

Locke laughed, unmoved by Cherrick's apprehension. He pushed Stumpf out of the way so as to face the old man, whose song-speech had now lowered in pitch; it was almost lilting. He was singing twilight, Stumpf thought: that brief ambiguity between the fierce day and the suffocating night. Yes, that was it. He could hear in the song the purr and the coo of a drowsy kingdom. It was so persuasive he wanted to lie down on the spot where he stood, and sleep.

Locke broke the spell. 'What are you saying?' he spat in the tribesman's mazy face. 'Talk sense!'

But the night-noises only whispered on, an unbroken stream.

'This is our village,' another voice now broke in; the man spoke as if translating the elder's words. Locke snapped round to locate the speaker. He was a thin youth, whose skin might once have been golden. '*Our* village. *Our* land.'

'You speak English,' Locke said.

'Some,' the youth replied.

'Why didn't you answer me earlier?' Locke demanded, his fury exacerbated by the disinterest on the Indian's face.

'Not my place to speak,' the man replied. 'He is the elder.'

'The Chief, you mean?'

'The Chief is dead. All his family is dead. This is the wisest of us –'

'Then you tell him –'

'No need to tell,' the young man broke in. 'He understands you.'

'He speaks English too?'

'No,' the other replied, 'but he understands you. You are . . . transparent.'

Locke half-grasped that the youth was implying an insult here, but wasn't quite certain. He gave Stumpf a puzzled look. The German shook his head. Locke returned his attention to the youth. 'Tell him anyway,' he said, 'tell all of them. This is our land. We bought it.'

'The tribe has always lived here,' the reply came.

'Not any longer,' Cherrick said.

'We've got papers –' Stumpf said mildly, still hoping that the confrontation might end peacefully, '– from the government.'

'We were here before the government,' the tribesman replied.

The old man had stopped talking the forest. Perhaps, Stumpf thought, he's coming to the beginning of another day, and stopped. He was turning away now, indifferent to the presence of these unwelcome guests.

'Call him back,' Locke demanded, stabbing his rifle towards the young tribesman. The gesture was unambiguous. 'Make him tell the rest of them they've got to go.'

The young man seemed unimpressed by the threat of Locke's rifle, however, and clearly unwilling to give orders to his elder, whatever the imperative. He simply watched the old man walk back towards the hut from which he had emerged. Around the compound, others were also turning away. The old man's withdrawal apparently signalled that the show was over.

'*No!*' said Cherrick, 'you're not *listening*.' The colour in his cheeks had risen a tone; his voice, an octave. He pushed forward, rifle raised. '*You fucking scum!*'

Despite his hysteria, he was rapidly losing his audience. The old man had reached the doorway of his hut, and now bent his back and disappeared into its recesses; the few members of the tribe who were still showing some interest in proceedings were viewing the Europeans with a hint of pity for their lunacy. It only enraged Cherrick further.

'Listen to me!' he shrieked, sweat flicking off his brow as he jerked his head at one retreating figure and then at another. '*Listen*, you bastards.'

'Easy . . .' said Stumpf.

The appeal triggered Cherrick. Without warning he raised his rifle to his shoulder, aimed at the open door of the hut into which the old man had vanished and fired. Birds rose from the crowns of adjacent trees; dogs took to their heels. From within the hut came a tiny shriek, not like the old man's voice at all. As it sounded, Stumpf fell to his knees, hugging his belly, his gut in spasm. Face to the ground, he did not see the diminutive figure emerge from the hut and totter into the sunlight. Even when he did look up, and saw how the child with the

61

scarlet face clutched his belly, he hoped his eyes lied. But they did not. It was blood that came from between the child's tiny fingers, and death that had stricken his face. He fell forward on to the impacted earth of the hut's threshold, twitched, and died.

Somewhere amongst the huts a woman began to sob quietly. For a moment the world spun on a pin-head, balanced exquisitely between silence and the cry that must break it, between a truce held and the coming atrocity.

'You stupid bastard,' Locke murmured to Cherrick. Under his condemnation, his voice trembled. 'Back off,' he said. 'Get up, Stumpf. We're not waiting. Get up and come now, or don't come at all.'

Stumpf was still looking at the body of the child. Suppressing his moans, he got to his feet.

'Help me,' he said. Locke lent him an arm. 'Cover us,' he said to Cherrick.

The man nodded, deathly-pale. Some of the tribe had turned their gaze on the Europeans' retreat, their expressions, despite this tragedy, as inscrutable as ever. Only the sobbing woman, presumably the dead child's mother, wove between the silent figures, keening her grief.

Cherrick's rifle shook as he kept the bridgehead. He'd done the mathematics; if it came to a head-on collision they had little chance of survival. But even now, with the enemy making a getaway, there was no sign of movement amongst the Indians. Just the accusing facts: the dead boy; the warm rifle. Cherrick chanced a look over his shoulder. Locke and Stumpf were already within twenty yards of the jeep, and there was still no move from the savages.

Then, as he looked back towards the compound, it seemed as though the tribe breathed together one solid breath, and hearing that sound Cherrick felt death wedge itself like a fish-bone in his throat, too deep to be plucked out by his fingers, too big to be shat. It was just waiting there, lodged in his anatomy, beyond argument or appeal. He was distracted from its presence by a movement at the door of the hut. Quite ready to make the same mistake again, he took firmer hold of his rifle. The old man had re-appeared at the door. He stepped over the corpse of the boy, which was lying where it had toppled. Again, Cherrick glanced behind him. Surely they were at the jeep? But Stumpf had stumbled; Locke was even now dragging him to his feet. Cherrick, seeing the old man advancing towards him, took one cautious step backwards, followed by another. But the old man was fearless. He walked swiftly across the compound coming to stand so close to Cherrick, his body as vulnerable as ever, that the barrel of the rifle prodded his shrunken belly.

There was blood on both his hands, fresh enough to run down the man's arms when he displayed the palms for Cherrick's benefit. Had he touched the boy, Cherrick wondered, as he stepped out of the hut? If so, it had been an astonishing sleight-of-hand, for Cherrick had seen nothing. Trick or no trick, the significance of the display was perfectly apparent: he was being accused of murder. Cherrick wasn't about to be cowed, however. He stared back at the old man, matching defiance with defiance.

But the old bastard did nothing, except show his bloody palms, his eyes full of tears. Cherrick could feel his anger growing again. He poked the man's flesh with his finger.

'You don't frighten me,' he said, 'you understand? I'm not a fool.'

As he spoke he seemed to see a shifting in the old man's features. It was a trick of the sun, of course, or of bird-shadow, but there was, beneath the corruption of age, a hint of the child now dead at the hut door: the tiny mouth even seemed to smile. Then, as subtly as it had appeared, the illusion faded again.

Cherrick withdrew his hand from the old man's chest, narrowing his eyes against further mirages. He then renewed his retreat. He had taken three steps only when something broke cover to his left. He swung round, raised his rifle and fired. A piebald pig, one of several that had been grazing around the huts, was checked in its flight by the bullet, which struck it in the neck. It seemed to trip over itself, and collapsed headlong in the dust.

Cherrick swung his rifle back towards the old man. But he hadn't moved, except to open his mouth. His palate was making the sound of the dying pig. A choking squeal, pitiful and ridiculous, which followed Cherrick back up the path to the jeep. Locke had the engine running. 'Get in,' he said. Cherrick needed no encouragement, but flung himself into the front seat. The interior of the vehicle was filthy hot, and stank of Stumpf's bodily functions, but it was as near safety as they'd been in the last hour.

'It was a pig,' he said, 'I shot a pig.'

'I saw,' said Locke.

'That old bastard . . .'

He didn't finish. He was looking down at the two fingers with which he had prodded the elder. 'I touched him,' he muttered, perplexed by what he saw. The fingertips were bloody, though the flesh he had laid his fingers upon had been clean.

Locke ignored Cherrick's confusion and backed the jeep up to turn it around, then drove away from the hamlet, down a track that seemed to have become choked with foliage in the hour since they'd come up it. There was no discernible pursuit.

The tiny trading post to the south of Averio was scant of civilisation, but it sufficed. There were white faces here, and clean water. Stumpf, whose condition had deteriorated on the return journey, was treated by Dancy, an Englishman who had the manner of a disenfranchised earl and a face like hammered steak. He claimed to have been a doctor once upon a sober time, and though he had no evidence of his qualifications nobody contested his right to deal with Stumpf. The German was delirious, and on occasion violent, but Dancy, his small hands heavy with gold rings, seemed to take a positive delight in nursing his thrashing patient.

While Stumpf raved beneath his mosquito net, Locke and Cherrick sat in the lamp-lit gloom and drank, then told the story of their encounter with the tribe. It was Tetelman, the owner of the trading post's stores, who had most to say when the report was finished. He knew the Indians well.

'I've been here years,' he said, feeding nuts to the mangy monkey that scampered on his lap. 'I know the way these people think. They may act as though they're stupid; cowards even. Take it from me, they're neither.'

Cherrick grunted. The quicksilver monkey fixed him with vacant eyes. 'They didn't make a move on us,' Cherrick said, 'even though they outnumbered us ten to one. If that isn't cowardice, what is it?'

Tetelman settled back in his creaking chair, throwing the animal off his lap. His face was raddled and used. Only his lips, constantly rewetted from his glass, had any colour; he looked, thought Locke, like an old whore.

'Thirty years ago,' Tetelman said, 'this whole territory was their homeland. Nobody wanted it; they *went* where they liked, *did* what they liked. As far as we whites were concerned the jungle was filthy and disease-infected: we wanted no part of it. And, of course, in some ways we were right. It *is* filthy and disease-infected; but it's also got reserves we now want badly: minerals, oil maybe: power.'

'We paid for that land,' said Locke, his fingers jittery on the cracked rim of his glass. 'It's all we've got now.'

Tetelman sneered. 'Paid?' he said. The monkey chattered at his feet, apparently as amused by this claim as its master. 'No. You just paid for a blind eye, so you could take it by force. You paid for the right to fuck up the Indians in any way you could. That's what your dollars bought, Mr Locke. The government of this country is counting off the months until every tribe on the sub-continent is wiped out by you or your like. It's no use to play the outraged innocents. I've been here too long . . .'

Cherrick spat on to the bare floor. Tetelman's speech had heated his blood.

'And so why'd *you* come here, if you're so fucking clever?' he asked the trader.

'Same reason as you,' Tetelman replied plainly, staring off into the trees beyond the plot of land behind the store. Their silhouettes shook against the sky; wind, or night-birds.

'What reason's that?' Cherrick said, barely keeping his hostility in check.

'Greed,' Tetelman replied mildly, still watching the trees. Something scampered across the low wooden roof. The monkey at Tetelman's feet listened, head cocked. 'I thought I could make my fortune out here, the same way you do. I gave myself two years. Three at the most.

That was the best part of two decades ago.' He frowned; whatever thoughts passed behind his eyes, they were bitter. 'The jungle eats you up and spits you out, sooner or later.'

'Not me,' said Locke.

Tetelman turned his eyes on the man. They were wet. 'Oh yes,' he said politely. 'Extinction's in the air, Mr Locke. I can smell it.' Then he turned back to looking at the window.

Whatever was on the roof now had companions.

'They won't come here, will they?' said Cherrick. 'They won't follow us?'

The question, spoken almost in a whisper, begged for a reply in the negative. Try as he might Cherrick couldn't dislodge the sights of the previous day. It wasn't the boy's corpse that so haunted him; that he could soon learn to forget. But the elder – with his shifting, sunlit face – and the palms raised as if to display some stigmata, he was not so forgettable.

'Don't fret,' Tetelman said, with a trace of condescension. 'Sometimes one or two of them will drift in here with a parrot to sell, or a few pots, but I've never seen them come here in any numbers. They don't like it. This is civilisation as far as they're concerned, and it intimidates them. Besides, they wouldn't harm my guests. They need me.'

'Need you?' said Locke; who could need this wreck of a man?

'They use our medicines. Dancy supplies them. And blankets, once in a while. As I said, they're not so stupid.'

Next door, Stumpf had begun to howl. Dancy's consoling voice could be heard, attempting to talk down the panic. He was plainly failing.

'Your friend's gone bad,' said Tetelman.

'No friend,' Cherrick replied.

'It rots,' Tetelman murmured, half to himself.

'What does?'

'The soul.' The word was utterly out of place from Tetelman's whisky-glossed lips. 'It's like fruit, you see. It rots.'

Somehow Stumpf's cries gave force to the observation. It was not the voice of a wholesome creature; there was putrescence in it.

More to direct his attention away from the German's din than out of any real interest, Cherrick said: 'What do they give you for the medicine and the blankets? Women?'

The possibility clearly entertained Tetelman; he laughed, his gold teeth gleaming. 'I've no use for women,' he said. 'I've had the syph for too many years.' He clicked his fingers and the monkey clambered back up on to his lap. 'The soul,' he said, 'isn't the only thing that rots.'

'Well, what do you get from them then?' Locke said. 'For your supplies?'

'Artifacts,' Tetelman replied. 'Bowls, jugs, mats. The Americans buy them off me, and sell them again in Manhattan. Everybody wants something made by an extinct tribe these days. *Memento mori*.'

'Extinct?' said Locke. The word had a seductive ring; it sounded like life to him.

'Oh certainly,' said Tetelman. 'They're as good as gone. If you don't wipe them out, they'll do it themselves.'

'Suicide?' Locke said.

'In their fashion. They just lose heart. I've seen it happen half a dozen times. A tribe loses its land, and its appetite for life goes with it. They stop taking care of themselves. The women don't get pregnant any more;

68

the young men take to drink, the old men just starve themselves to death. In a year or two it's like they never existed.'

Locke swallowed the rest of his drink, silently saluting the fatal wisdom of these people. They knew when to die, which was more than could be said for some he'd met. The thought of their death-wish absolved him of any last vestiges of guilt. What was the gun in his hand, except an instrument of evolution?

On the fourth day after their arrival at the post, Stumpf's fever abated, much to Dancy's disappointment. 'The worst of it's over,' he announced. 'Give him two more days' rest and you can get back to your labours.'

'What are your plans?' Tetelman wanted to know.

Locke was watching the rain from the verandah. Sheets of water pouring from clouds so low they brushed the tree-tops. Then, just as suddenly as it had arrived, the downpour was gone, as though a tap had been turned off. Sun broke through; the jungle, new-washed, was steaming and sprouting and thriving again.

'I don't know what we'll do,' said Locke. 'Maybe get ourselves some help and go back in there.'

'There are ways,' Tetelman said.

Cherrick, sitting beside the door to get the benefit of what little breeze was available, picked up the glass that had scarcely been out of his hand in recent days, and filled it up again. 'No more guns,' he said. He hadn't touched his rifle since they'd arrived at the post; in fact he kept from contact with anything but a bottle and his bed. His skin seemed to crawl and creep perpetually.

'No need for guns,' Tetelman murmured. The statement hung on the air like an unfulfilled promise.

'Get rid of them without guns?' said Locke. 'If you mean waiting for them to die out naturally, I'm not that patient.'

'No,' said Tetelman, 'we can be swifter than that.'

'How?'

Tetelman gave the man a lazy look. 'They're my livelihood,' he said, 'or part of it. You're asking me to help you make myself bankrupt.'

He not only looks like an old whore, Locke thought, he thinks like one. 'What's it worth? Your wisdom?' he asked.

'A cut of whatever you find on your land,' Tetelman replied.

Locke nodded. 'What have we got to lose? Cherrick? You agree to cut him in?' Cherrick's consent was a shrug. 'All right,' Locke said, 'talk.'

'They need medicines,' Tetelman explained, 'because they're so susceptible to our diseases. A decent plague can wipe them out practically overnight.'

Locke thought about this, not looking at Tetelman. 'One fell swoop,' Tetelman continued. 'They've got practically no defences against certain bacteria. Never had to build up any resistance. The clap. Smallpox. Even measles.'

'How?' said Locke.

Another silence. Down the steps of the verandah, where civilization finished, the jungle was swelling to meet the sun. In the liquid heat plants blossomed and rotted and blossomed again.

'I asked *how*,' Locke said.

'Blankets,' Tetelman replied, 'dead men's blankets.'

A little before the dawn of the night after Stumpf's recovery, Cherrick woke suddenly, startled from his rest by bad dreams. Outside it was pitch-dark; neither

70

moon nor stars relieved the depth of the night. But his body-clock, which his life as a mercenary had trained to impressive accuracy, told him that first light was not far off, and he had no wish to lay his head down again and sleep. Not with the old man waiting to be dreamt. It wasn't just the raised palms, the blood glistening, that so distressed Cherrick. It was the words he'd dreamt coming from the old man's toothless mouth which had brought on the cold sweat that now encased his body.

What were the words? He couldn't recall them now, but wanted to; wanted the sentiments dragged into wakefulness, where they could be dissected and dismissed as ridiculous. They wouldn't come though. He lay on his wretched cot, the dark wrapping him up too tightly for him to move, and suddenly the bloody hands were there, in front of him, suspended in the pitch. There was no face, no sky, no tribe. Just the hands.

'Dreaming,' Cherrick told himself, but he knew better.

And now, the voice. He was getting his wish; here were the words he had dreamt spoken. Few of them made sense. Cherrick lay like a newborn baby, listening to its parents talk but unable to make any significance of their exchanges. He was ignorant, wasn't he? He tasted the sourness of his stupidity for the first time since childhood. The voice made him fearful of ambiguities he had ridden roughshod over, of whispers his shouting life had rendered inaudible. He fumbled for comprehension, and was not entirely frustrated. The man was speaking of the world, and of exile from the world; of being broken always by what one seeks to possess. Cherrick struggled, wishing he could stop the voice and ask for explanation. But it was already fading, ushered away by the wild address of parrots in the trees,

71

raucous and gaudy voices erupting suddenly on every side. Through the mesh of Cherrick's mosquito net he could see the sky flaring through the branches.

He sat up. Hands and voice had gone; and with them all but an irritating murmur of what he had almost understood. He had thrown off in sleep his single sheet; now he looked down at his body with distaste. His back and buttocks, and the underside of his thighs, felt sore. Too much sweating on coarse sheets, he thought. Not for the first time in recent days he remembered a small house in Bristol which he had once known as home.

The noise of birds was filling his head. He hauled himself to the edge of the bed and pulled back the mosquito net. The crude weave of the net seemed to scour the palm of his hand as he gripped it. He disengaged his hold, and cursed to himself. There was again today an itch of tenderness in his skin that he'd suffered since coming to the post. Even the soles of his feet, pressed on to the floor by the weight of his body, seemed to suffer each knot and splinter. He wanted to be away from this place, and badly.

A warm trickle across his wrist caught his attention, and he was startled to see a rivulet of blood moving down his arm from his hand. There was a cut in the cushion of his thumb, where the mosquito net had apparently nicked his flesh. It was bleeding, though not copiously. He sucked at the cut, feeling again that peculiar sensitivity to touch that only drink, and that in abundance, dulled. Spitting out blood, he began to dress.

The clothes he put on were a scourge to his back. His sweat-stiffened shirt rubbed against his shoulders and neck; he seemed to feel every thread chafing his nerve-endings. The shirt might have been sackcloth, the way it abraded him.

Next door, he heard Locke moving around. Gingerly finishing his dressing, Cherrick went through to join him. Locke was sitting at the table by the window. He was poring over a map of Tetelman's, and drinking a cup of the bitter coffee Dancy was so fond of brewing, which he drank with a dollop of condensed milk. The two men had little to say to each other. Since the incident in the village all pretence to respect or friendship had disappeared. Locke now showed undisguised contempt for his sometime companion. The only fact that kept them together was the contract they and Stumpf had signed. Rather than breakfast on whisky, which he knew Locke would take as a further sign of his decay, Cherrick poured himself a slug of Dancy's emetic and went out to look at the morning.

He felt strange. There was something about this dawning day which made him profoundly uneasy. He knew the dangers of courting unfounded fears, and he tried to forbid them, but they were incontestable.

Was it simply exhaustion that made him so painfully conscious of his many discomforts this morning? Why else did he feel the pressure of his stinking clothes so acutely? The rasp of his boot collar against the jutting bone of his ankle, the rhythmical chafing of his trousers against his inside leg as he walked, even the grazing air that eddied around his exposed face and arms. The world was pressing on him – at least that was the sensation – pressing as though it wanted him out.

A large dragonfly, whining towards him on iridescent wings, collided with his arm. The pain of the collision caused him to drop his mug. It didn't break, but rolled off the verandah and was lost in the undergrowth. Angered, Cherrick slapped the insect off, leaving a

73

smear of blood on his tattooed forearm to mark the dragonfly's demise. He wiped it off. It welled up again on the same spot, full and dark.

It wasn't the blood of the insect, he realised, but his own. The dragonfly had cut him somehow, though he had felt nothing. Irritated, he peered more closely at his punctured skin. The wound was not significant, but it *was* painful.

From inside he could hear Locke talking. He was loudly describing the inadequacy of his fellow adventures to Tetelman.

'Stumpf's not fit for this kind of work,' he was saying. 'And Cherrick –'

'What about me?'

Cherrick stepped into the shabby interior, wiping a new flow of blood from his arm.

Locke didn't even bother to look up at him. 'You're paranoid,' he said plainly. 'Paranoid and unreliable.'

Cherrick was in no mood for taking Locke's foul-mouthing. 'Just because I killed some Indian brat,' he said. The more he brushed blood from his bitten arm, the more the place stung. 'You just didn't have the balls to do it yourself.'

Locke still didn't bother to look up from his perusal of the map. Cherrick moved across to the table.

'Are you listening to me?' he demanded, and added force to his question by slamming his fist down on to the table. On impact his hand simply burst open. Blood spurted out in every direction, spattering the map.

Cherrick howled, and reeled backwards from the table with blood pouring from a yawning split in the side of his hand. The bone showed. Through

74

the din of pain in his head he could hear a quiet voice. The words were inaudible, but he knew whose they were.

'I won't hear!' he said, shaking his head like a dog with a flea in its ear. He staggered back against the wall, but the briefest of contacts was another agony. *I won't hear, damn you!*

'What the hell's he talking about?' Dancy had appeared in the doorway, woken by the cries, still clutching the *Complete Works of Shelley* Tetelman had said he could not sleep without.

Locke re-addressed the question to Cherrick, who was standing, wild-eyed, in the corner of the room, blood spitting from between his fingers as he attempted to staunch his wounded hand. 'What are you saying?'

'He spoke to me,' Cherrick replied. 'The old man.'

'What old man?' Tetelman asked.

'He means at the village,' Locke said. Then, to Cherrick, 'Is that what you mean?'

'He wants us out. Exiles. Like them. *Like them!*' Cherrick's panic was rapidly rising out of anyone's control, least of all his own.

'The man's got heat-stroke,' Dancy said, ever the diagnostician. Locke knew better.

'Your hand needs bandaging . . .' he said, slowly approaching Cherrick.

'I heard him . . .' Cherrick muttered.

'I believe you. Just slow down. We can sort it out.'

'No,' the other man replied. 'It's pushing us out. Everything we touch. Everything we touch.'

He looked as though he was about to topple over, and Locke reached for him. As his hands made contact with Cherrick's shoulders the flesh beneath the shirt split, and Locke's hands were instantly soaked in scarlet. He withdrew them, appalled. Cherrick fell to his knees, which in their turn became new wounds. He stared down as his shirt and trousers darkened. 'What's happening to me?' he wept.

Dancy moved towards him. 'Let me help.'

'No! Don't touch me!' Cherrick pleaded, but Dancy wasn't to be denied his nursing.

'It's all right,' he said in his best bedside manner.

It wasn't. Dancy's grip, intended only to lift the man from his bleeding knees, opened new cuts wherever he took hold. Dancy felt the blood sprout beneath his hand, felt the flesh slip away from the bone. The sensation bested even his taste for agony. Like Locke, he forsook the lost man.

'He's rotting,' he murmured.

Cherrick's body had split now in a dozen or more places. He tried to stand, half staggering to his feet only to collapse again, his flesh breaking open whenever he touched wall or chair or floor. There was no help for him. All the others could do was stand around like spectators at an execution, awaiting the final throes. Even Stumpf had roused himself from his bed and come through to see what all the shouting was about. He stood leaning against the door-lintel, his disease-thinned face all disbelief.

Another minute, and blood-loss defeated Cherrick. He keeled over and sprawled, face down, across the floor. Dancy crossed back to him and crouched on his haunches beside his head.

'Is he dead?' Locke asked.

'Almost,' Dancy replied.

'Rotted,' said Tetelman, as though the word explained the atrocity they had just witnessed. He had a crucifix in his hand, large and crudely carved. It looked like Indian handiwork, Locke thought. The Messiah impaled on the

76

tree was sloe-eyed and indecently naked. He smiled, despite nail and thorn.

Dancy touched Cherrick's body, letting the blood come with his touch, and turned the man over, then leaned in towards Cherrick's jittering face. The dying man's lips were moving, oh so slightly.

'What are you saying?' Dancy asked; he leaned closer still to catch the man's words. Cherrick's mouth trailed bloody spittle, but no sound came.

Locke stepped in, pushing Dancy aside. Flies were already flitting around Cherrick's face. Locke thrust his bull-necked head into Cherrick's view. 'You hear me?' he said.

The body grunted.

'You know me?'

Again, a grunt.

'You want to give me your share of the land?'

The grunt was lighter this time; almost a sigh.

'There's witnesses here,' Locke said. 'Just say yes. They'll hear you. Just say yes.'

The body was trying its best. It opened its mouth a little wider.

'Dancy —' said Locke. 'You hear what he said?'

Dancy could not disguise his horror at Locke's insistence, but he nodded.

'You're a witness.'

'If you must,' said the Englishman.

Deep in his body Cherrick felt the fish-bone he'd first choked on in the village twist itself about one final time, and extinguish him.

'Did he say yes, Dancy?' Tetelman asked.

Dancy felt the physical proximity of the brute kneeling beside him. He didn't know what the dead man had said, but what did it matter? Locke would have the land anyway, wouldn't he?

77

'He said yes.'

Locke stood up, and went in search of a fresh cup of coffee.

Without thinking, Dancy put his fingers on Cherrick's lids to seal his empty gaze. Under that lightest of touches the lids broke open and blood tainted the tears that had swelled where Cherrick's sight had been.

They had buried him towards evening. The corpse, though it had lain through the noon-heat in the coolest part of the store, amongst the dried goods, had begun to putrefy by the time it was sewn up in canvas for the burial. The night following, Stumpf had come to Locke and offered him the last third of the territory to add to Cherrick's share, and Locke, ever the realist, had accepted. The terms, which were punitive, had been worked out the next day. In the evening of that day, as Stumpf had hoped, the supply plane came in. Locke, bored with Tetelman's contemptuous looks, had also elected to fly back to Santarem, there to drink the jungle out of his system for a few days, and return refreshed. He intended to buy up fresh supplies, and, if possible, hire a reliable driver and gunman.

The flight was noisy, cramped and tedious; the two men exchanged no words for its full duration. Stumpf just kept his eyes on the tracts of unfelled wilderness they passed over, though from one hour to the next the scene scarcely changed. A panorama of sable green, broken on occasion by a glint of water; perhaps a column of blue smoke rising here and there, where land was being cleared; little else.

At Santarem they parted with a single handshake which left every nerve in Stumpf's hand scourged, and an open cut in the tender flesh between index finger and thumb.

★

Santarem wasn't Rio, Locke mused as he made his way down to a bar at the south end of the town, run by a veteran of Vietnam who had a taste for ad hoc animal shows. It was one of Locke's few certain pleasures, and one he never tired of, to watch a local woman, face dead as a cold manioc cake, submit to a dog or a donkey for a few grubby dollar bills. The women of Santarem were, on the whole, as unpalatable as the beer, but Locke had no eye for beauty in the opposite sex: it mattered only that their bodies be in reasonable working order, and not diseased. He found the bar, and settled down for an evening exchanging dirt with the American. When he tired of that – some time after midnight – he bought a bottle of whisky and went out looking for a face to press his heat upon.

The woman with the squint was about to accede to a particular peccadillo of Locke's – one which she had resolutely refused until drunkenness persuaded her to abandon what little hope of dignity she had – when there came a rap on the door.

'Fuck,' said Locke.

'*Si*,' said the woman. 'Fook. Fook.' It seemed to be the only word she knew in anything resembling English. Locke ignored her and crawled drunkenly to the edge of the stained mattress. Again, the rap on the door.

'Who is it?' he said.

'*Senhor* Locke?' The voice from the hallway was that of a young boy.

'Yes?' said Locke. His trousers had become lost in the tangle of sheets. 'Yes? What do you want?'

'*Mensagem*,' the boy said. '*Urgente. Urgente.*'

'For me?' He had found his trousers, and was pulling them on. The woman, not at all disgruntled by this desertion, watched him from the head of the bed, toying with an empty bottle. Buttoning up, Locke crossed from bed to door, a matter of three steps. He unlocked it. The boy in the darkened hallway was of Indian extraction to judge by the blackness of his eyes, and that peculiar lustre his skin owned. He was dressed in a T-shirt bearing the Coca-Cola motif.

'*Mensagem, Senhor* Locke,' he said again, '. . . *do hospital.*'

The boy was staring past Locke at the woman on the bed. He grinned from ear to ear at her cavortings.

'Hospital?' said Locke.

'*Sim. Hospital "Sacrado Coraçã de Maria".*'

It could only be Stumpf, Locke thought. Who else did he know in this corner of Hell who'd call upon him? Nobody. He looked down at the leering child.

'*Vem comigo,*' the boy said, '*vem comigo. Urgente.*'

'No,' said Locke. 'I'm not coming. Not now. You understand? Later. Later.'

The boy shrugged. '. . . *Tá morrendo,*' he said.

'Dying?' said Locke.

'*Sim. Tá morrendo.*'

'Well, let him. Understand me? You go back, and tell him, I won't come until I'm ready.'

Again, the boy shrugged. '*E meu dinheiro?*' he said, as Locke went to close the door.

'You go to Hell,' Locke replied, and slammed it in the child's face.

When, two hours and one ungainly act of passionless sex later, Locke unlocked the door, he discovered that the child, by way of revenge, had defecated on the threshold.

The hospital '*Sacrado Coraçã de Maria*' was no place to fall ill; better, thought Locke, as he made his way down the dingy corridors, to die in your own bed with your

80

own sweat for company than come here. The stench of disinfectant could not entirely mask the odour of human pain. The walls were ingrained with it; it formed a grease on the lamps, it slickened the unwashed floors. What had happened to Stumpf to bring him here? a bar-room brawl, an argument with a pimp about the price of a woman? The German was just damn fool enough to get himself stuck in the gut over something so petty. '*Senhor* Stumpf?' he asked of a woman in white he accosted in the corridor. 'I'm looking for *Senhor* Stumpf.'

The woman shook her head, and pointed towards a harried-looking man further down the corridor, who was taking a moment to light a small cigar. He let go the nurse's arm and approached the fellow. He was enveloped in a stinking cloud of smoke.

'I'm looking for *Senhor* Stumpf,' he said.

The man peered at him quizzically.

'You are Locke?' he asked.

'Yes.'

'Ah.' He drew on the cigar. The pungency of the expelled smoke would surely have brought on a relapse in the hardiest patient. 'I'm Doctor Edson Costa,' the man said, offering his clammy hand to Locke. 'Your friend has been waiting for you to come all night.'

'What's wrong with him?'

'He's hurt his eye,' Edson Costa replied, clearly indifferent to Stumpf's condition. 'And he has some minor abrasions on his hands and face. But he won't have anyone go near him. He doctored himself.'

'Why?' Locke asked.

The doctor looked flummoxed. 'He pays to go in a clean room. Pays plenty. So I put him in. You want to see him? Maybe take him away?'

'Maybe,' said Locke, unenthusiastically.

'His head . . .' said the doctor. 'He has delusions.'

Without offering further explanation, the man led off at a considerable rate, trailing tobacco-smoke as he went. The route, that wound out of the main building and across a small internal courtyard, ended at a room with a glass partition in the door.

'Here,' said the doctor. 'Your friend. You tell him,' he said as a parting snipe, 'he pay more, or tomorrow he leaves.'

Locke peered through the glass partition. The grubby-white room was empty, but for a bed and a small table, lit by the same dingy light that cursed every wretched inch of this establishment. Stumpf was not on the bed, but squatting on the floor in the corner of the room. His left eye was covered with a bulbous padding, held in place by a bandage ineptly wrapped around his head.

Locke was looking at the man for a good time before Stumpf sensed that he was watched. He looked up slowly. His good eye, as if in compensation for the loss of its companion, seemed to have swelled to twice its natural size. It held enough fear for both it and its twin; indeed enough for a dozen eyes.

Cautiously, like a man whose bones are so brittle he fears an injudicious breath will shatter them, Stumpf edged up the wall, and crossed to the door. He did not open it, but addressed Locke through the glass.

'Why didn't you come?' he said.

'I'm here.'

'But *sooner*,' said Stumpf. His face was raw, as if he'd been beaten. 'Sooner.'

'I had business,' Locke returned. 'What happened to you?'

'It's true, Locke,' the German said, 'everything is true.'

'What are you talking about?'

'Tetelman told me. Cherrick's babblings. About being exiles. It's true. They mean to drive us out.'

'We're not in the jungle now,' Locke said. 'You've got nothing to be afraid of here.'

'Oh yes,' said Stumpf, that wide eye wider than ever. 'Oh yes! I saw him –'

'Who?'

'The elder. From the village. He was here.'

'Ridiculous.'

'*He was here*, damn you,' Stumpf replied. 'He was standing where you're standing. Looking at me through the glass.'

'You've been drinking too much.'

'It happened to Cherrick, and now it's happening to me. They're making it impossible to live –'

Locke snorted. 'I'm not having any problem,' he said.

'They won't let you escape,' Stumpf said. 'None of us'll escape. Not unless we make amends.'

'You've got to vacate the room,' Locke said, unwilling to countenance any more of this drivel. 'I've been told you've got to get out by morning.'

'No,' said Stumpf. 'I can't leave. I can't leave.'

'There's nothing to fear.'

'The dust,' said the German. 'The dust in the air. It'll cut me up. I got a speck in my eye – just a *speck* – and the next thing my eye's bleeding as though it'll never stop. I can't hardly lie down, the sheet's like a bed of nails. The soles of my feet feel as if they're going to split. You've got to help me.'

'How?' said Locke.

'Pay them for the room. Pay them so I can stay 'til you can get a specialist from Sao Luis. Then go back to the village, Locke. Go back and tell them. I don't want the land. Tell them I don't own it any longer.'

'I'll go back,' said Locke, 'but in my good time.'

'You must go *quickly*,' said Stumpf. 'Tell them to let me be.'

Suddenly, the expression on the partially-masked face changed, and Stumpf looked past Locke at some spectacle down the corridor. From his mouth, slack with fear, came the small word, 'Please.'

Locke, mystified by the man's expression, turned. The corridor was empty, except for the fat moths that were besetting the bulb. 'There's nothing there –' he said, turning back to the door of Stumpf's room. The wire-mesh glass of the window bore the distinct imprint of two bloody palms.

'He's here,' the German was saying, staring fixedly at the miracle of the bleeding glass. Locke didn't need to ask who. He raised his hand to touch the marks. The handprints, still wet, were on *his* side of the glass, not on Stumpf's.

'My God,' he breathed. How could anyone have slipped between him and the door and laid the prints there, sliding away again in the brief moment it had taken him to glance behind him? It defied reason. Again he looked back down the corridor. It was still bereft of visitors. Just the bulb – swinging slightly, as if a breeze of passage had caught it – and the moth's wings, whispering. 'What's happening?' Locke breathed.

Stumpf, entranced by the handprints, touched his fingertips lightly to the glass. On contact, his fingers blossomed blood, trails of which idled down the glass. He didn't remove his fingers, but stared through at Locke with despair in his eye.

'See?' he said, very quietly.

'What are you playing at?' Locke said, his voice similarly hushed. 'This is some kind of trick.'

'No.'

'You haven't got Cherrick's disease. You can't have. You didn't touch them. We *agreed*, damn you,' he said, more heatedly. 'Cherrick touched them, *we didn't*.'

Stumpf looked back at Locke with something close to pity on his face.

'We were wrong,' he said gently. His fingers, which he had now removed from the glass, continued to bleed, dribbling across the backs of his hands and down his arms. 'This isn't something you can beat into submission, Locke. It's out of our hands.' He raised his bloody fingers, smiling at his own word-play: 'See?' he said.

The German's sudden, fatalistic calm frightened Locke. He reached for the handle of the door, and jiggled it. The room was locked. The key was on the inside, where Stumpf had paid for it to be.

'Keep out,' Stumpf said. 'Keep away from me.'

His smile had vanished. Locke put his shoulder to the door.

'Keep out, I said,' Stumpf shouted, his voice shrill. He backed away from the door as Locke took another lunge at it. Then, seeing that the lock must soon give, he raised a cry of alarm. Locke took no notice, but continued to throw himself at the door. There came the sound of wood beginning to splinter.

Somewhere nearby Locke heard a woman's voice, raised in response to Stumpf's calls. No matter; he'd have his hands on the German before help could come, and then, by Christ, he'd wipe every last vestige of a smile from the bastard's lips. He threw himself against the door with increased fervour; again, and again. The door gave.

In the antiseptic cocoon of his room Stumpf felt the first blast of unclean air from the outside world. It was no more than a light breeze that invaded his

makeshift sanctuary, but it bore upon its back the
debris of the world. Soot and seeds, flakes of skin
itched off a thousand scalps, fluff and sand and twists
of hair; the bright dust from a moth's wing. Motes so
small the human eye only glimpsed them in a shaft
of white sunlight; each a tiny, whirling speck quite
harmless to most living organisms. But this cloud was
lethal to Stumpf; in seconds his body became a field of
tiny, seeping wounds.

He screeched, and ran towards the door to slam it
closed again, flinging himself into a hail of minute razors,
each lacerating him. Pressing against the door to prevent
Locke from entering, his wounded hands erupted. He
was too late to keep Locke out anyhow. The man had
pushed the door wide, and was now stepping through,
his every movement setting up further currents of air to
cut Stumpf down. He snatched hold of the German's
wrist. At his grip the skin opened as if beneath a knife.

Behind him, a woman loosed a cry of horror. Locke,
realizing that Stumpf was past recanting his laughter,
let the man go. Adorned with cuts on every exposed
part of his body, and gaining more by the moment,
Stumpf stumbled back, blind, and fell beside the bed.
The killing air still sliced him as he sank down; with each
agonised shudder he woke new eddies and whirlpools to
open him up.

Ashen, Locke retreated from where the body lay, and
staggered out into the corridor. A gaggle of onlookers
blocked it; they parted, however, at his approach, too
intimidated by his bulk and by the wild look on his
face to challenge him. He retraced his steps through the
sickness-perfumed maze, crossing the small courtyard
and returning into the main building. He briefly caught
sight of Edson Costa hurrying in pursuit, but did not
linger for explanations.

In the vestibule, which, despite the late hour was busy with victims of one kind or another, his harried gaze alighted on a small boy, perched on his mother's lap. He had injured his belly apparently. His shirt, which was too large for him, was stained with blood; his face with tears. The mother did not look up as Locke moved through the throng. The child did however. He raised his head as if knowing that Locke was about to pass by, and smiled radiantly.

There was nobody Locke knew at Tetelman's store; and all the information he could bully from the hired hands, most of whom were drunk to the point of being unable to stand, was that their masters had gone off into the jungle the previous day. Locke chased the most sober of them and persuaded him with threats to accompany him back to the village as translator. He had no real idea of how he would make his peace with the tribe. He was only certain that he had to argue his innocence. After all, he would plead, it hadn't been *he* who had fired the killing shot. There had been misunderstandings, to be certain, but he had not harmed the people in any way. How could they, in all conscience, conspire to hurt him? If they should require some penance of him he was not above acceding to their demands. Indeed, might there not be some satisfaction in the act? He had seen so much suffering of late. He wanted to be cleansed of it. Anything they asked, within reason, he would comply with; anything to avoid dying like the others. He'd even give back the land.

It was a rough ride, and his morose companion complained often and incoherently. Locke turned a deaf ear. There was no time for loitering. Their noisy progress, the jeep engine complaining at every new acrobatic required of it, brought the jungle alive on every side, a repertoire of wails, whoops and screeches. It was an urgent, hungry place, Locke thought: and for the first time since setting foot on this sub-continent he loathed it with all his heart. There was no room here to make sense of events; the best that could be hoped was that one be allowed a niche to breathe awhile between one squalid flowering and the next.

Half an hour before nightfall, exhausted by the journey, they came to the outskirts of the village. The place had altered not at all in the meagre days since he'd last been here, but the ring of huts was clearly deserted. The doors gaped; the communal fires, always alight, were ashes. There was neither child nor pig to turn an eye towards him as he moved across the compound. When he reached the centre of the ring he stood still, looking about him for some clue as to what had happened there. He found none, however. Fatigue made him foolhardy. Mustering his fractured strength, he shouted into the hush:

'*Where are you?*'

Two brilliant red macaws, finger-winged, rose screeching from the trees on the far side of the village. A few moments after, a figure emerged from the thicket of balsa and jacaranda. It was not one of the tribe, but Dancy. He paused before stepping fully into sight; then, recognising Locke, a broad smile broke his face, and he advanced into the compound. Behind him, the foliage shook as others made their way through it. Tetelman was there, as were several Norwegians, led by a man called Bjørnstrøm, whom Locke had encountered briefly at the trading post. His face, beneath a shock of sun-bleached hair, was like cooked lobster.

'My God,' said Tetelman, 'what are you doing here?'

'I might ask you the same question,' Locke replied testily.

Bjørnstrøm waved down the raised rifles of his three companions and strode forward, bearing a placatory smile.

'Mr Locke,' the Norwegian said, extending a leather-gloved hand. 'It is good we meet.'

Locke looked down at the stained glove with disgust, and Bjørnstrøm, flashing a self-admonishing look, pulled it off. The hand beneath was pristine.

'My apologies,' he said. 'We've been working.'

'At what?' Locke asked, the acid in his stomach edging its way up into the back of his throat.

Tetelman spat. 'Indians,' he said.

'Where's the tribe?' Locke said.

Again, Tetelman: 'Bjørnstrøm claims he's got rights to this territory . . .'

'The tribe,' Locke insisted. 'Where are they?'

The Norwegian toyed with his glove.

'Did you buy them out, or what?' Locke asked.

'Not exactly,' Bjørnstrøm replied. His English, like his profile, was impeccable.

'Bring him along,' Dancy suggested with some enthusiasm. 'Let him see for himself.'

Bjørnstrøm nodded. 'Why not?' he said. 'Don't touch anything, Mr Locke. And tell your carrier to stay where he is.'

Dancy had already about turned, and was heading into the thicket; now Bjørnstrøm did the same, escorting Locke across the compound towards a corridor hacked through the heavy foliage. Locke could scarcely keep pace; his limbs were more reluctant with every step he took. The ground had been heavily trodden along this track. A litter of leaves and orchid blossoms had been mashed into the sodden soil.

They had dug a pit in a small clearing no more than a hundred yards from the compound. It was not deep, this pit, nor was it very large. The mingled smells of lime and petrol cancelled out any other scent.

Tetelman, who had reached the clearing ahead of Locke, hung back from approaching the lip of the earthworks, but Dancy was not so fastidious. He strode around the far side of the pit and beckoned to Locke to view the contents.

The tribe were putrefying already. They lay where they had been thrown, in a jumble of breasts and buttocks and faces and limbs, their bodies tinged here and there with purple and black. Flies built helter-skelters in the air above them.

'An education,' Dancy commented.

Locke just looked on as Bjørnstrøm moved around the other side of the pit to join Dancy.

'All of them?' Locke asked.

The Norwegian nodded. 'One fell swoop,' he said, pronouncing each word with unsettling precision.

'Blankets,' said Tetelman, naming the murder weapon.

'But so quickly . . .' Locke murmured.

'It's very efficient,' said Dancy. 'And difficult to prove. Even if anybody ever asks.'

'Disease is natural,' Bjørnstrøm observed. 'Yes? Like the trees.'

Locke slowly shook his head, his eyes pricking.

'I hear good things of you,' Bjørnstrøm said to him. 'Perhaps we can work together.'

Locke didn't even attempt to reply. Others of the Norwegian party had laid down their rifles and were now getting back to work, moving the few bodies still to be pitched amongst their fellows from the forlorn heap beside the pit. Locke could see a child amongst the tangle, and an old man, whom even now the burial party were picking up. The corpse looked jointless as they

90

swung it over the edge of the hole. It tumbled down the shallow incline and came to rest face up, its arms flung up to either side of its head in a gesture of submission, or expulsion. It was the elder of course, whom Cherrick had faced. His palms were still red. There was a neat bullet-hole in his temple. Disease and hopelessness had not been entirely efficient, apparently.

Locke watched while the next of the bodies was thrown into the mass grave, and a third to follow that.

Bjørnstrøm, lingering on the far side of the pit, was lighting a cigarette. He caught Locke's eye.

'So it goes,' he said.

From behind Locke, Tetelman spoke.

'We thought you wouldn't come back,' he said, perhaps attempting to excuse his alliance with Bjørnstrøm.

'Stumpf is dead,' said Locke.

'Well, even less to divide up,' Tetelman said, approaching him and laying a hand on his shoulder. Locke didn't reply; he just stared down amongst the bodies, which were now being covered with lime, only slowly registering the warmth that was running down his body from the spot where Tetelman had touched him. Disgusted, the man had removed his hand, and was staring at the growing bloodstain on Locke's shirt.

TWILIGHT AT
THE TOWERS

THE PHOTOGRAPHS OF Mironenko which Ballard had been shown in Munich had proved far from instructive. Only one or two pictured the KGB man full face; and of the others most were blurred and grainy, betraying their furtive origins. Ballard was not overmuch concerned. He knew from long and occasionally bitter experience that the eye was all too ready to be deceived; but there were other faculties – the remnants of senses modern life had rendered obsolete – which he had learned to call into play, enabling him to sniff out the least signs of betrayal. These were the talents he would use when he met with Mironenko. With them, he would root the truth from the man.

The truth? Therein lay the conundrum of course, for in this context wasn't sincerity a movable feast? Sergei Zakharovich Mironenko had been a Section Leader in Directorate S of the KGB for eleven years, with access to the most privileged information on the dispersal of Soviet Illegals in the West. In the recent weeks, however, he had made his disenchantment with his present masters, and his consequent desire to defect, known to the British Security Service. In return for the elaborate efforts which would have to be made on his behalf he had volunteered to act as an agent within the KGB for a period of three months, after which time he would be taken into the bosom of democracy and hidden where his vengeful overlords would never find him. It had fallen to Ballard to meet the Russian face to face, in the hope of establishing whether Mironenko's disaffection from his ideology was real or faked. The answer would not be found on Mironenko's lips, Ballard knew, but in some behavioural nuance which only instinct would comprehend.

Time was when Ballard would have found the puzzle fascinating; that his every waking thought would have circled on the unravelling ahead. But such commitment had belonged to a man convinced his actions had some significant effect upon the world. He was wiser now. The agents of East and West went about their secret works year in, year out. They plotted; they connived; occasionally (though rarely) they shed blood. There were débâcles and trade-offs and minor tactical victories. But in the end things were much the same as ever.

This city, for instance. Ballard had first come to Berlin in April of 1969. He'd been twenty-nine, fresh from years of intensive training, and ready to live a little. But he had not felt easy here. He found the city charmless; often bleak. It had taken Odell, his colleague for those first two years, to prove that Berlin was worthy of his affections, and once Ballard fell he was lost for life. Now he felt more at home in this divided city than he ever had in London. Its unease, its failed idealism, and – perhaps most acutely of all – its terrible isolation, matched his. He and it, maintaining a presence in a wasteland of dead ambition.

He found Mironenko at the Germälde Galerie, and yes, the photographs *had* lied. The Russian looked older than his forty-six years, and sicker than he'd appeared in those filched portraits. Neither man made any sign of acknowledgement. They idled through the collection for a full half-hour, with Mironenko showing acute, and apparently genuine, interest in the work on view. Only when both men were satisfied that they were not being watched did the Russian quit the building and lead Ballard into the polite suburbs of Dahlem to a mutually agreed safe house. There, in a small and unheated kitchen, they sat down and talked.

Mironenko's command of English was uncertain, or at least appeared so, though Ballard had the impression that his struggles for sense were as much tactical as grammatical. He might well have presented the same façade in the Russian's situation; it seldom hurt to appear less competent than one was. But despite the difficulties he had in expressing himself, Mironenko's avowals were unequivocal.

'I am no longer a Communist,' he stated plainly, 'I have not been a party-member – not *here* –' he put his fist to his chest '– for many years.'

He fetched an off-white handkerchief from his coat pocket, pulled off one of his gloves, and plucked a bottle of tablets from the folds of the handkerchief.

'Forgive me,' he said as he shook tablets from the bottle. 'I have pains. In my head; in my hands.'

Ballard waited until he had swallowed the medication before asking him, 'Why did you begin to doubt?'

The Russian pocketed the bottle and the handkerchief, his wide face devoid of expression.

94

'How does a man lose his . . . his faith?' he said. 'Is it that I saw too much; or too little, perhaps?'

He looked at Ballard's face to see if his hesitant words had made sense. Finding no comprehension there he tried again.

'I think the man who does not believe he is lost, is lost.'

The paradox was elegantly put; Ballard's suspicion as to Mironenko's true command of English was confirmed.

'Are you lost *now*?' Ballard inquired.

Mironenko didn't reply. He was pulling his other glove off and staring at his hands. The pills he had swallowed did not seem to be easing the ache he had complained of. He fisted and unfisted his hands like an arthritis sufferer testing the advance of his condition. Not looking up, he said:

'I was taught that the Party had solutions to everything. That made me free from fear.'

'And now?'

'Now?' he said. 'Now I have strange thoughts. They come to me from nowhere . . .'

'Go on,' said Ballard.

Mironenko made a tight smile. 'You must know me inside out, yes? Even what I dream?'

'Yes,' said Ballard.

Mironenko nodded. 'It would be the same with us,' he said. Then, after a pause: 'I've thought sometimes I would break open. Do you understand what I say? I would crack, because there is such rage inside me. And that makes me afraid, Ballard. I think they will see how much I hate them.' He looked up at his interrogator. 'You must be quick,' he said, 'or they will discover me. I try not to think of what they will do.' Again, he paused. All trace of the smile, however humourless, had gone. 'The Directorate has Sections even I don't have knowledge of. Special hospitals, where nobody can go. They have ways to break a man's soul in pieces.'

Ballard, ever the pragmatist, wondered if Mironenko's vocabulary wasn't rather high-flown. In the hands of the KGB he doubted if he would be thinking of his *soul*'s contentment. After all, it was the body that had the nerve-endings.

They talked for an hour or more, the conversation moving back and forth between politics and personal reminiscence, between trivia and confessional. At the end of the meeting Ballard was in no doubt as to Mironenko's antipathy to his masters. He was, as he had said, a man without faith.

The following day Ballard met with Cripps in the restaurant at the Schweizerhof Hotel, and made his verbal report on Mironenko.

'He's ready and waiting. But he insists we be quick about making up our minds.'

'I'm sure he does,' Cripps said. His glass eye was troubling him today; the chilly air, he explained, made it sluggish. It moved fractionally more slowly than his real eye, and on occasion Cripps had to nudge it with his fingertip to get it moving.

'We're not going to rushed into any decision,' Cripps said.

'Where's the problem? I don't have any doubt about his commitment; or his desperation.'

'So you said,' Cripps replied. 'Would you like something for dessert?'

'Do you doubt my appraisal? Is that what it is?'

'Have something sweet to finish off, so that I don't feel an utter reprobate.'

'You think I'm wrong about him, don't you?' Ballard pressed. When Cripps didn't reply, Ballard leaned across the table. 'You do, don't you?'

'I'm just saying there's reason for caution,' Cripps said. 'If we finally choose to take him on board the Russians are going to be very distressed. We have to be sure the deal's worth the bad weather that comes with it. Things are so dicey at the moment.'

'When aren't they?' Ballard replied. 'Tell me a time when there wasn't some crisis in the offing?' He settled back in the chair and tried to read Cripps' face. His glass eye was, if anything, more candid than the real one.

'I'm sick of this damn game,' Ballard muttered.

The glass eye roved. 'Because of the Russian?'

'Maybe.'

'Believe me,' said Cripps, 'I've got good reason to be careful with this man.'

'Name one.'

'There's nothing verified.'

'What have you got on him?' Ballard insisted.

'As I say, rumour,' Cripps replied.

'Why wasn't I briefed about it?'

Cripps made a tiny shake of his head. 'It's academic now,' he said. 'You've provided a good report. I just want you to understand that if things don't go the way you think they should it's not because your appraisals aren't trusted.'

'I see.'

'No you don't,' said Cripps. 'You're feeling martyred; and I don't altogether blame you.'

'So what happens now? I'm supposed to forget I ever met the man?'

'Wouldn't do any harm,' said Cripps. 'Out of sight, out of mind.'

★

Clearly Cripps didn't trust Ballard to take his own advice. Though Ballard made several discreet enquiries about the Mironenko case in the following week it was plain that his usual circle of contacts had been warned to keep their lips sealed.

As it was, the next news about the case reached Ballard via the pages of the morning papers, in an article about a body found in a house near the station on Kaiser Damm. At the time of reading he had no way of knowing how the account tied up with Mironenko, but there was enough detail in the story to arouse his interest. For one, he had the suspicion that the house named in the article had been used by the Service on occasion; for another, the article described how two unidentified men had almost been caught in the act of removing the body, further suggesting that this was no crime of passion.

About noon, he went to see Cripps at his offices in the hope of coaxing him with some explanation, but Cripps was not available, nor would be, his secretary explained, until further notice; matters arising had taken him back to Munich. Ballard left a message that he wished to speak with him when he returned.

As he stepped into the cold air again, he realised that he'd gained an admirer; a thin-faced individual whose hair had retreated from his brow, leaving a ludicrous forelock at the high-water mark. Ballard knew him in passing from Cripps' entourage but couldn't put a name to the face. It was swiftly provided.

'Suckling,' the man said.

'Of course,' said Ballard. 'Hello.'

'I think maybe we should talk, if you have a moment,' the man said. His voice was as pinched as his features; Ballard wanted none of his gossip. He was about to refuse the offer when Suckling said: 'I suppose you heard what happened to Cripps.'

Ballard shook his head. Suckling, delighted to possess this nugget, said again: 'We should talk.'

They walked along the Kantstrasse towards the Zoo. The street was busy with lunchtime pedestrians, but Ballard scarcely noticed them. The story that Suckling unfolded as they walked demanded his full and absolute attention.

It was simply told. Cripps, it appeared, had made an arrangement to meet with Mironenko in order to make his own assessment of the Russian's integrity. The house in Schöneberg chosen for the meeting had been used on several previous occasions, and had long been considered one of the safest locations in the city. It had not proved so the previous evening however. KGB men had apparently followed Mironenko to the house, and then attempted to break the party up. There was nobody to testify to what had happened subsequently – both the men who had accompanied Cripps, one of them Ballard's old colleague Odell – were dead; Cripps himself was in a coma.

'And Mironenko?' Ballard inquired.

Suckling shrugged. 'They took him home to the Motherland, presumably,' he said.

Ballard caught a whiff of deceit off the man.

'I'm touched that you're keeping me up to date,' he said to Suckling. 'But *why*?'

'You and Odell were friends, weren't you?' came the reply. 'With Cripps out of the picture you don't have many of those left.'

'Is that so?'

'No offence intended,' Suckling said hurriedly. 'But you've got a reputation as a maverick.'

'Get to the point,' said Ballard.

'There is no point,' Suckling protested. 'I just thought you ought to know what had happened. I'm putting my neck on the line here.'

'Nice try,' said Ballard. He stopped walking. Suckling wandered on a pace or two before turning to find Ballard grinning at him.

'Who sent you?'

'Nobody sent me,' Suckling said.

'Clever to send the court gossip. I almost fell for it. You're very plausible.'

There wasn't enough fat on Suckling's face to hide the tic in his cheek.

'What do they suspect me of? Do they think I'm conniving with Mironenko, is that it? No, I don't think they're that stupid.'

Suckling shook his head, like a doctor in the presence of some incurable disease. 'You like making enemies?' he said.

'Occupational hazard. I wouldn't lose any sleep over it. I don't.'

'There's changes in the air,' Suckling said. 'I'd make sure you have your answers ready.'

'Fuck the answers,' Ballard said courteously. 'I think it's about time I worked out the right questions.'

Sending Suckling to sound him out smacked of desperation. They wanted inside information; but about what? Could they seriously believe he had some involvement with Mironenko; or worse, with the KGB itself? He let his resentment subside; it was stirring up too much mud, and he needed clear water if he was to find his way free of this confusion. In one regard, Suckling was perfectly correct: he *did* have enemies, and with Cripps indisposed he was vulnerable. In such circumstances there were two courses of action.

100

He could return to London, and there lie low, or wait around in Berlin to see what manoeuvre they tried next. He decided on the latter. The charm of hide-and-seek was rapidly wearing thin.

As he turned North onto Leibnizstrasse he caught the reflection of a grey-coated man in a shop window. It was a glimpse, no more, but he had the feeling that he knew the fellow's face. Had they put a watch-dog onto him, he wondered? He turned, and caught the man's eye, holding it. The suspect seemed embarrassed, and looked away. A performance perhaps; and then again, perhaps not. It mattered little, Ballard thought. Let them watch him all they liked. He was guiltless. If indeed there was such a condition this side of insanity.

A strange happiness had found Sergei Mironenko; happiness that came without rhyme or reason, and filled his heart up to overflowing.

Only the previous day circumstances had seemed unendurable. The aching in his hands and head and spine had steadily worsened, and was now accompanied by an itch so demanding he'd had to snip his nails to the flesh to prevent himself doing serious damage. His body, he had concluded, was in revolt against him. It was that thought which he had tried to explain to Ballard: that he was divided from himself, and feared that he would soon be torn apart. But today the fear had gone.

Not so the pains. They were, if anything, worse than they'd been yesterday. His sinews and ligaments ached as if they'd been exercised beyond the limits of their design; there were bruises at all his joints, where blood had broken its banks beneath the skin. But that sense of imminent rebellion had disappeared, to be replaced with a dreamy peacefulness. And at its heart, such happiness.

When he tried to think back over recent events, to work out what had cued this transformation, his memory played tricks. He had been called to meet with Ballard's superior; *that* he remembered. Whether he had gone to the meeting, he did not. The night was a blank.

Ballard would know how things stood, he reasoned. He had liked and trusted the Englishman from the beginning, sensing that despite the many differences between them they were more alike than not. If he let his instinct lead, he would find Ballard, of that he was certain. No doubt the Englishman would be surprised to see him; even angered at first. But when he told Ballard of this new-found happiness surely his trespasses would be forgiven?

Ballard dined late, and drank until later still in The Ring, a small transvestite bar which he had been first taken to by Odell almost two decades ago. No doubt his guide's intention had been to prove his sophistication by showing his raw colleague the decadence of Berlin, but Ballard, though he never felt any sexual *frisson* in the company of The Ring's clientele, had immediately felt at home here. His neutrality was respected; no attempts were made to solicit him. He was simply left to drink and watch the passing parade of genders.

Coming here tonight raised the ghost of Odell, whose name would now be scrubbed from conversation because of his involvement with the Mironenko affair. Ballard had seen this process at work before. History did not forgive failure, unless it was so profound as to achieve a kind of grandeur. For the Odells of the world – ambitious men who had found themselves through little fault of their own in a cul-de-sac from which all retreat was barred – for such men there would be no fine words spoken nor medals struck. There would only be oblivion.

It made him melancholy to think of this, and he drank heavily to keep his thoughts mellow, but when – at two in the morning – he stepped out on to the street his depression was only marginally dulled. The good burghers of Berlin were well a-bed; tomorrow was another working day. Only the sound of traffic from the Kurfürstendamm offered sign of life somewhere near. He made his way towards it, his thoughts fleecy.

Behind him, laughter. A young man – glamorously dressed as a starlet – tottered along the pavement arm in arm with his unsmiling escort. Ballard recognised the transvestite as a regular at the bar; the client, to judge by his sober suit, was an out-of-towner slaking his thirst for boys dressed as girls behind his wife's back. Ballard picked up his pace. The young man's laughter, its musicality patently forced, set his teeth on edge.

He heard somebody running nearby; caught a shadow moving out of the corner of his eye. His watch-dog, most likely. Though alcohol had blurred his instincts, he felt some anxiety surface, the root of which he couldn't fix. He walked on. Featherlight tremors ran in his scalp.

A few yards on, he realised that the laughter from the street behind him had ceased. He glanced over his shoulder, half-expecting to see the boy and his customer embracing. But both had disappeared; slipped off down one of the alleyways, no doubt, to conclude their contract in darkness. Somewhere near, a dog had begun to bark wildly. Ballard turned round to look back the way he'd come, daring the deserted street to display its secrets to him. Whatever was arousing the buzz in his head and the itch on his palms, it was no commonplace anxiety. There was something wrong with the street, despite its show of innocence; it hid terrors.

The bright lights of the Kurfürstendamm were no more than three minutes' walk away, but he didn't want to turn his back on this mystery and take refuge there. Instead he proceeded to walk back the way he'd come, slowly. The dog had now ceased its alarm, and settled into silence; he had only his footsteps for company.

He reached the corner of the first alleyway and peered down it. No light burned at window or doorway. He could sense no living presence in the gloom. He crossed over the alley and walked on to the next. A luxurious stench had crept into the air, which became more lavish yet as he approached the corner. As he breathed it in the buzz in his head deepened to a threat of thunder.

A single light flickered in the throat of the alley, a meagre wash from an upper window. By it, he saw the body of the out-of-towner, lying sprawled on the ground. He had been so traumatically mutilated it seemed an attempt might have been made to turn him inside out. From the spilled innards, that ripe smell rose in all its complexity.

Ballard had seen violent death before, and thought himself indifferent to the spectacle. But something here in the alley threw his calm into disarray. He felt his limbs begin to shake. And then, from beyond the throw of light, the boy spoke.

'In God's name . . .' he said. His voice had lost all pretension to femininity; it was a murmur of undisguised terror.

Ballard took a step down the alley. Neither the boy, nor the reason for his whispered prayer, became visible until he had advanced ten yards. The boy was half-slumped against the wall amongst the refuse. His sequins and taffeta had been ripped from him; the body was pale and sexless. He seemed not to notice Ballard: his eyes were fixed on the deepest shadows.

The shaking in Ballard's limbs worsened as he followed the boy's gaze; it was all he could do to prevent his teeth from chattering. Nevertheless he continued his advance, not for the boy's sake (heroism had little merit, he'd always been taught) but because he was curious, more than curious, *eager*, to see what manner of man was capable of such casual violence. To look into the eyes of such ferocity seemed at that moment the most important thing in all the world.

Now the boy saw him, and muttered a pitiful appeal, but Ballard scarcely heard it. He felt other eyes upon him, and their touch was like a blow. The din in his head took on a sickening rhythm, like the sound of helicopter rotors. In mere seconds it mounted to a blinding roar.

Ballard pressed his hands to his eyes, and stumbled back against the wall, dimly aware that the killer was moving out of hiding (refuse was overturned) and making his escape. He felt something brush against him, and opened his eyes in time to glimpse the man slipping away down the passageway. He seemed somehow misshapen; his back crooked, his head too large. Ballard loosed a shout after him, but the berserker ran on, pausing only to look down at the body before racing towards the street.

Ballard heaved himself off the wall and stood upright. The noise in his head was diminishing somewhat; the attendant giddiness was passing.

Behind him, the boy had begun sobbing. 'Did you see?' he said. 'Did you *see*?'

'Who was it? Somebody you knew?'

The boy stared at Ballard like a frightened doe, his mascaraed eyes huge.

'Somebody . . .?' he said.

Ballard was about to repeat the question when there came a shriek of brakes, swiftly followed by the sound of the impact. Leaving the boy to pull his tattered *trousseau* about him, Ballard went back into the street. Voices were raised nearby; he hurried to their source. A large car was straddling the pavement, its headlights blazing. The driver was being helped from his seat, while his passengers – party-goers to judge by their dress and drink-flushed faces – stood and debated furiously as to how the accident had happened. One of the women was talking about an animal in the road, but another of the passengers corrected her. The body that lay in the gutter where it had been thrown was not that of an animal.

Ballard had seen little of the killer in the alleyway but he knew instinctively that this was he. There was no sign of the malformation he thought he'd glimpsed, however; just a man dressed in a suit that had seen better days, lying face down in a patch of blood. The police had already arrived, and an officer shouted to him to stand away from the body, but Ballard ignored the instruction and went to steal a look at the dead man's face. There was nothing there of the ferocity he had hoped so much to see. But there was much he recognised nevertheless.

The man was Odell.

He told the officers that he had seen nothing of the accident, which was essentially true, and made his escape from the scene before events in the adjacent alley were discovered.

It seemed every corner turned on his route back to his rooms brought a fresh question. Chief amongst them: why he had been lied to about Odell's death? And what psychosis had seized the man that made him capable of the slaughter Ballard had witnessed? He would not get the answers to these questions from his sometime colleagues, that he knew. The only man whom he might have beguiled an answer from was

Cripps. He remembered the debate they'd had about Mironenko, and Cripps' talk of 'reasons for caution' when dealing with the Russian. The Glass Eye had known then that there was something in the wind, though surely even he had not envisaged the scale of the present disaster. Two highly valued agents murdered; Mironenko missing, presumed dead; he himself – if Suckling was to be believed – at death's door. And all this begun with Sergei Zakharovich Mironenko, the lost man of Berlin. It seemed his tragedy was infectious.

Tomorrow, Ballard decided, he would find Suckling and squeeze some answers from him. In the meantime, his head and his hands ached, and he wanted sleep. Fatigue compromised sound judgement, and if ever he needed that faculty it was now. But despite his exhaustion sleep eluded him for an hour or more, and when it came it was no comfort. He dreamt whispers; and hard upon them, rising as if to drown them out, the roar of the helicopters. Twice he surfaced from sleep with his head pounding; twice a hunger to understand what the whispers were telling him drove him to the pillow again. When he woke for the third time, the noise between his temples had become crippling; a thought-cancelling assault which made him fear for his sanity. Barely able to see the room through the pain, he crawled from his bed.

'Please . . .' he murmured, as if there were somebody to help him from his misery.

A cool voice answered him out of the darkness:

'*What do you want?*'

He didn't question the questioner; merely said:

'Take the pain away.'

'*You can do that for yourself,*' the voice told him.

He leaned against the wall, nursing his splitting head, tears of agony coming and coming. 'I don't know *how*,' he said.

'*Your dreams give you pain,*' the voice replied, '*so you must forget them. Do you understand? Forget them, and the pain will go.*'

He understood the instruction, but not how to realise it. He had no powers of government in sleep. He was the object of these whispers; not they his. But the voice insisted.

'*The dream means you harm, Ballard. You must bury it. Bury it deep.*'

'Bury it?'

'*Make an image of it, Ballard. Picture it in detail.*'

He did as he was told. He imagined a burial party, and a box; and in the box, this dream. He made them dig deep, as the voice instructed him, so that he would never be able to disinter this hurtful thing again. But even as he imagined the box lowered into the pit he heard its boards creak. The dream would not lie down. It beat against confinement. The boards began to break.

'*Quickly!*' the voice said.

The din of the rotors had risen to a terrifying pitch. Blood had begun to pour from his nostrils; he tasted salt at the back of his throat.

'*Finish it!*' the voice yelled above the tumult. '*Cover it up!*'

Ballard looked into the grave. The box was thrashing from side to side.

'*Cover it, damn you!*'

He tried to make the burial party obey; tried to will them to pick up their shovels and bury the offending thing alive, but they would not. Instead they gazed into the grave as he did and watched as the contents of the box fought for light.

'*No!*' the voice demanded, its fury mounting. '*You must not look!*'

The box danced in the hole. The lid splintered. Briefly, Ballard glimpsed something shining up between the boards.

'*It will kill you!*' the voice said, and as if to prove its point the volume of the sound rose beyond the point of endurance, washing out burial party, box and all in a blaze of pain. Suddenly it seemed that what the voice said was true; that he was near to death. But it wasn't the dream that was conspiring to kill him, but the sentinel they had posted between him and it: this skull-splintering cacophony.

Only now did he realise that he'd fallen on the floor, prostrate beneath this assault. Reaching out blindly he found the wall, and hauled himself towards it, the machines still thundering behind his eyes, the blood hot on his face.

He stood up as best he could and began to move towards the bathroom. Behind him the voice, its tantrum controlled, began its exhortation afresh. It sounded so intimate that he looked round, fully expecting to see the speaker, and he was not disappointed. For a few flickering moments he seemed to be standing in a small, windowless room, its walls painted a uniform white. The light here was bright and dead, and in the centre of the room stood the face behind the voice, smiling.

'*Your dreams give you pain,*' he said. This was the first commandment again. '*Bury them Ballard, and the pain will pass.*'

Ballard wept like a child; this scrutiny shamed him. He looked away from his tutor to bury his tears.

'*Trust us,*' another voice said, close by. '*We're your friends.*'

He didn't trust their fine words. The very pain they claimed to want to save him from was of their making; it was a stick to beat him with if the dreams came calling.

'*We want to help you,*' one or other of them said.

'No . . .' he murmured. 'No damn you . . . I don't . . . I don't believe . . .'

The room flickered out, and he was in the bedroom again, clinging to the wall like a climber to a cliff-face. Before they could come for him with more words, more pain, he edged his way to the bathroom door, and stumbled blindly towards the shower. There was a moment of panic while he located the taps; and then the water came on at a rush. It was bitterly cold, but he put his head beneath it, while the onslaught of rotor-blades tried to shake the plates of his skull apart. Icy water trekked down his back, but he let the rain come down on him in a torrent, and by degrees, the helicopters took their leave. He didn't move, though his body juddered with cold, until the last of them had gone; then he sat on the edge of the bath, mopping water from his neck and face and body, and eventually, when his legs felt courageous enough, made his way back into the bedroom.

He lay down on the same crumpled sheets in much the same position as he'd lain in before; yet nothing *was* the same. He didn't know what had changed in him, or how. But he lay there without sleep disturbing his serenity through the remaining hours of the night, trying to puzzle it out, and a little before dawn he remembered the words he had muttered in the face of the delusion. Simple words; but oh, their power.

'I don't believe . . .' he said; and the commandments trembled.

It was half an hour before noon when he arrived at the small book exporting firm which served Suckling for cover. He felt quick-witted, despite the disturbance of the night, and rapidly charmed his way past the receptionist and entered Suckling's office unannounced. When Suckling's eyes settled on his visitor he started from his desk as if fired upon.

'Good morning,' said Ballard. 'I thought it was time we talked.'

Suckling's eyes fled to the office-door, which Ballard had left ajar.

'Sorry; is there a draught?' Ballard closed the door gently. 'I want to see Cripps,' he said.

Suckling waded through the sea of books and manuscripts that threatened to engulf his desk. 'Are you out of your mind, coming back here?'

'Tell them I'm a friend of the family,' Ballard offered.

'I can't believe you'd be so stupid.'

'Just point me to Cripps, and I'll be away.'

Suckling ignored him in favour of his tirade. 'It's taken two years to establish my credentials here.'

Ballard laughed.

'I'm going to report this, damn you!'

'I think you should,' said Ballard, turning up the volume. 'In the meanwhile: *where's Cripps*?'

Suckling, apparently convinced that he was faced with a lunatic, controlled his apoplexy. 'All right,' he said. 'I'll have somebody call on you; take you to him.'

'Not good enough,' Ballard replied. He crossed to Suckling in two short strides and took hold of him by his lapel. He'd spent at most three hours with Suckling in ten years, but he'd scarcely passed a moment in his presence without itching to do what he was doing now. Knocking the man's hands away, he pushed Suckling against the book-lined

111

wall. A stack of volumes, caught by Suckling's heel, toppled.

'Once more,' Ballard said. 'The old man.'

'Take your fucking hands off me,' Suckling said, his fury redoubled at being touched.

'Again,' said Ballard. '*Cripps.*'

'I'll have you carpeted for this. I'll have you *out*!'

Ballard leaned towards the reddening face, and smiled.

'I'm out anyway. People have died, remember? London needs a sacrificial lamb, and I think I'm it.' Suckling's face dropped. 'So I've got nothing to lose, have I?' There was no reply. Ballard pressed closer to Suckling, tightening his grip on the man. '*Have I?*'

Suckling's courage failed him. 'Cripps is dead,' he said.

Ballard didn't release his hold. 'You said the same about Odell –' he remarked. At the name, Suckling's eyes widened. '– And I saw him only last night,' Ballard said, 'out on the town.'

'You saw Odell?'

'Oh yes.'

Mention of the dead man brought the scene in the alleyway back to mind. The smell of the body; the boy's sobs. There were other faiths, thought Ballard, beyond the one he'd once shared with the creature beneath him. Faiths whose devotions were made in heat and blood, whose dogmas were dreams. Where better to baptise himself into that new faith than here, in the blood of the enemy?

Somewhere, at the very back of his head, he could hear the helicopters, but he wouldn't let them take to the air. He was strong today; his head, his hands, all *strong*. When he drew his nails towards Suckling's eyes the blood came easily. He had a sudden vision of the face

112

beneath the flesh; of Suckling's features stripped to the essence.

'Sir?'

Ballard glanced over his shoulder. The receptionist was standing at the open door.

'Oh. I'm sorry,' she said, preparing to withdraw. To judge by her blushes she assumed this was a lover's tryst she'd walked in upon.

'*Stay*,' said Suckling. 'Mr Ballard . . . was just leaving.'

Ballard released his prey. There would be other opportunities to have Suckling's life.

'I'll see you again,' he said.

Suckling drew a handkerchief from his top pocket and pressed it to his face.

'Depend upon it,' he replied.

Now they would come for him, he could have no doubt of that. He was a rogue element, and they would strive to silence him as quickly as possible. The thought did not distress him. Whatever they had tried to make him forget with their brain-washing was more ambitious than they had anticipated; however deeply they had taught him to bury it, it was digging its way back to the surface. He couldn't see it yet, but he knew it was near. More than once on his way back to his rooms he imagined eyes at his back. Maybe he was still being tailed; but his instincts informed him otherwise. The presence he felt close-by – so near that it was sometimes at his shoulder – was perhaps simply another part of him. He felt protected by it, as by a local god.

He had half expected there to be a reception committee awaiting him at his rooms, but there was nobody. Either Suckling had been obliged to delay his alarm-call, or else the upper echelons were still debating

113

their tactics. He pocketed those few keepsakes that he wanted to preserve from their calculating eyes, and left the building again without anyone making a move to stop him.

It felt good to be alive, despite the chill that rendered the grim streets grimmer still. He decided, for no particular reason, to go to the zoo, which, though he had been visiting the city for two decades, he had never done. As he walked it occurred to him that he'd never been as free as he was now; that he had shed mastery like an old coat. No wonder they feared him. They had good reason.

Kantstrasse was busy, but he cut his way through the pedestrians easily, almost as if they sensed a rare certainty in him and gave him a wide berth. As he approached the entrance to the zoo, however, somebody jostled him. He looked round to upbraid the fellow, but caught only the back of the man's head as he was submerged in the crowd heading onto Hardenbergstrasse. Suspecting an attempted theft, he checked his pockets, to find that a scrap of paper had been slipped into one. He knew better than to examine it on the spot, but casually glanced round again to see if he recognised the courier. The man had already slipped away.

He delayed his visit to the zoo and went instead to the Tiergarten, and there – in the wilds of the great park – found a place to read the message. It was from Mironenko, and it requested a meeting to talk of a matter of considerable urgency, naming a house in Marienfelde as a venue. Ballard memorised the details, then shredded the note.

It was perfectly possible that the invitation was a trap of course, set either by his own faction or by the opposition. Perhaps a way to test his allegiance; or to manipulate him into a situation in which he could be easily despatched. Despite such doubts he had no choice but to go however, in the hope that this blind date was indeed with Mironenko. Whatever dangers this rendezvous brought, they were not so new. Indeed, given his long-held doubts of the efficacy of sight, hadn't every date he'd ever made been in some sense *blind*?

By early evening the damp air was thickening towards a fog, and by the time he stepped off the bus on Hildburghauserstrasse it had a good hold on the city, lending the chill new powers to discomfort.

Ballard went quickly through the quiet streets. He scarcely knew the district at all, but its proximity to the Wall bled it of what little charm it might once have possessed. Many of the houses were unoccupied; of those that were not most were sealed off against the night and the cold and the lights that glared from the watch-towers. It was only with the aid of a map that he located the tiny street Mironenko's note had named.

No lights burned in the house. Ballard knocked hard, but there was no answering footstep in the hall. He had anticipated several possible scenarios, but an absence of response at the house had not been amongst them. He knocked again; and again. It was only then that he heard sounds from within, and finally the door was opened to him. The hallway was painted grey and brown, and lit only by a bare bulb. The man silhouetted against this drab interior was not Mironenko.

'Yes?' he said. 'What do you want?' His German was spoken with a distinct Muscovite inflection.

'I'm looking for a friend of mine,' Ballard said.

The man, who was almost as broad as the doorway he stood in, shook his head.

'There's nobody here,' he said. 'Only me.'

'I was told –'

'You must have the wrong house.'

No sooner had the doorkeeper made the remark than noise erupted from down the dreary hallway. Furniture was being overturned; somebody had begun to shout.

The Russian looked over his shoulder and went to slam the door in Ballard's face, but Ballard's foot was there to stop him. Taking advantage of the man's divided attention, Ballard put his shoulder to the door, and pushed. He was in the hallway – indeed he was half-way down it – before the Russian took a step in pursuit. The sound of demolition had escalated, and was now drowned out by the sound of a man squealing. Ballard followed the sound past the sovereignty of the lone bulb and into gloom at the back of the house. He might well have lost his way at that point but that a door was flung open ahead of him.

The room beyond had scarlet floorboards; they glistened as if freshly painted. And now the decorator appeared in person. His torso had been ripped open from neck to navel. He pressed his hands to the breached dam, but they were useless to stem the flood; his blood came in spurts, and with it, his innards. He met Ballard's gaze, his eyes full to overflowing with death, but his body had not yet received the instruction to lie down and die; it juddered on in a pitiful attempt to escape the scene of execution behind him.

The spectacle had brought Ballard to a halt, and the Russian from the door now took hold of him, and pulled him back into the hallway, shouting into his face. The outburst, in panicked Russian, was beyond Ballard, but he needed no translation of the hands that encircled his throat. The Russian was half his weight again, and had the grip of an expert strangler, but Ballard felt effortlessly the man's superior. He wrenched the

116

attacker's hands from his neck, and struck him across the face. It was a fortuitous blow. The Russian fell back against the staircase, his shouts silenced.

Ballard looked back towards the scarlet room. The dead man had gone, though scraps of flesh had been left on the threshold.

From within, laughter.

Ballard turned to the Russian.

'What in God's name's going on?' he demanded, but the other man simply stared through the open door.

Even as he spoke, the laughter stopped. A shadow moved across the blood-splattered wall of the interior, and a voice said:

'Ballard?'

There was a roughness there, as if the speaker had been shouting all day and night, but it was the voice of Mironenko.

'Don't stand out in the cold,' he said, 'come on in. And bring Solomonov.'

The other man made a bid for the front door, but Ballard had hold of him before he could take two steps.

'There's nothing to be afraid of, Comrade,' said Mironenko. 'The dog's gone.' Despite the reassurance, Solomonov began to sob as Ballard pressed him towards the open door.

Mironenko was right; it *was* warmer inside. And there no sign of a dog. There was blood in abundance, however. The man Ballard had last seen teetering in the doorway had been dragged back into this abattoir while he and Solomonov had struggled. The body had been treated with astonishing barbarity. The head had been smashed open; the innards were a grim litter underfoot.

Squatting in the shadowy corner of this terrible room, Mironenko. He had been mercilessly beaten to judge by the swelling about his head and upper

117

torso, but his unshaven face bore a smile for his saviour.

'I knew you'd come,' he said. His gaze fell upon Solomonov. 'They followed me,' he said. 'They meant to kill me, I suppose. Is that what you intended, Comrade?'

Solomonov shook with fear – his eyes flitting from the bruised moon of Mironenko's face to the pieces of gut that lay everywhere about – finding nowhere a place of refuge.

'What stopped them?' Ballard asked.

Mironenko stood up. Even this slow movement caused Solomonov to flinch.

'Tell Mr Ballard,' Mironenko prompted. 'Tell him what happened.' Solomonov was too terrified to speak. 'He's KGB, of course,' Mironenko explained. 'Both trusted men. But not trusted enough to be warned, poor idiots. So they were sent to murder me with just a gun and a prayer.' He laughed at the thought. 'Neither of which were much use in the circumstances.'

'I beg you . . .' Solomonov murmured, '. . . let me go. I'll say nothing.'

'You'll say what they want you to say, Comrade, the way we all must,' Mironenko replied. 'Isn't that right, Ballard? All slaves of our faith?'

Ballard watched Mironenko's face closely; there was a fullness there that could not be entirely explained by the bruising. The skin almost seemed to crawl.

'They have made us forgetful,' Mironenko said.

'Of what?' Ballard enquired.

'Of ourselves,' came the reply, and with it Mironenko moved from his murky corner and into the light.

What had Solomonov and his dead companion done to him? His flesh was a mass of tiny contusions, and there were bloodied lumps at his neck and temples which Ballard might have taken for bruises but that they palpitated, as if something nested beneath the skin. Mironenko made no sign of discomfort however, as he reached out to Solomonov. At his touch the failed assassin lost control of his bladder, but Mironenko's intentions were not murderous. With eerie tenderness he stroked a tear from Solomonov's cheek. 'Go back to them,' he advised the trembling man. 'Tell them what you've seen.'

Solomonov seemed scarcely to believe his ears, or else suspected – as did Ballard – that this forgiveness was a sham, and that any attempt to leave would invite fatal consequences.

But Mironenko pressed his point. 'Go on,' he said. 'Leave us please. Or would you prefer to stay and eat?'

Solomonov took a single, faltering step towards the door. When no blow came he took a second step, and a third, and now he was out of the door and away.

'Tell them!' Mironenko shouted after him. The front door slammed.

'Tell them what?' said Ballard.

'That I've remembered,' Mironenko said. 'That I've found the skin they stole from me.'

For the first time since entering this house, Ballard began to feel queasy. It was not the blood nor the bones underfoot, but a look in Mironenko's eyes. He'd seen eyes as bright once before. But where?

'You –' he said quietly, 'you did this.'

'Certainly,' Mironenko replied.

'How?' Ballard said. There was a familiar thunder climbing from the back of his head. He tried to ignore it, and press some explanation from the Russian. 'How, damn you?'

119

'We are the same,' Mironenko replied. 'I smell it in you.'

'No,' said Ballard. The clamour was rising.

'The doctrines are just words. It's not what we're taught but what we *know* that matters. In our marrow; in our souls.'

He had talked of souls once before; of places his masters had built in which a man could be broken apart. At the time Ballard had thought such talk mere extravagance; now he wasn't so sure. What was the burial party all about, if not the subjugation of some secret part of him? The marrow-part; the soul-part.

Before Ballard could find the words to express himself, Mironenko froze, his eyes gleaming more brightly than ever.

'They're outside,' he said.

'Who are?'

The Russian shrugged. 'Does it matter?' he said. 'Your side or mine. Either one will silence us if they can.'

That much was true.

'We must be quick,' he said, and headed for the hallway. The front door stood ajar. Mironenko was there in moments. Ballard followed. Together they slipped out on to the street.

The fog had thickened. It idled around the street-lamps, muddying their light, making every doorway a hiding place. Ballard didn't wait to tempt the pursuers out into the open, but followed Mironenko, who was already well ahead, swift despite his bulk. Ballard had to pick up his pace to keep the man in sight. One moment he was visible, the next the fog closed around him.

The residential property they moved through now gave way to more anonymous buildings, warehouses perhaps, whose walls stretched up into the murky darkness unbroken by windows. Ballard called after him to slow his crippling pace. The Russian halted and turned back to Ballard, his outline wavering in the besieged light. Was it a trick of the fog, or had Mironenko's condition deteriorated in the minutes since they'd left the house? His face seemed to be seeping; the lumps on his neck had swelled further.

'We don't have to run,' Ballard said. 'They're not following.'

'They're always following,' Mironenko replied, and as if to give weight to the observation Ballard heard fog-deadened footsteps in a nearby street.

'No time to debate,' Mironenko murmured, and turning on his heel, he ran. In seconds, the fog had spirited him away again.

Ballard hesitated another moment. Incautious as it was, he wanted to catch a glimpse of his pursuers so as to know them for the future. But now, as the soft pad of Mironenko's step diminished into silence, he realised that the other footsteps had also ceased. Did they know he was waiting for them? He held his breath, but there was neither sound nor sign of them. The delinquent fog idled on. He seemed to be alone in it. Reluctantly, he gave up waiting and went after the Russian at a run.

A few yards on the road divided. There was no sign of Mironenko in either direction. Cursing his stupidity in lingering behind, Ballard followed the route which was most heavily shrouded in fog. The street was short, and ended at a wall lined with spikes, beyond which there was a park of some kind. The fog clung more tenaciously to this space of damp earth than it did to the street, and Ballard could see no more than four or five yards across the grass from where he stood. But he knew intuitively that he had chosen the right road; that Mironenko had scaled this wall and was waiting for him somewhere

121

close by. Behind him, the fog kept its counsel. Either their pursuers had lost him, or their way, or both. He hoisted himself up on to the wall, avoiding the spikes by a whisper, and dropped down on the opposite side.

The street had seemed pin-drop quiet, but it clearly wasn't, for it was quieter still inside the park. The fog was chillier here, and pressed more insistently upon him as he advanced across the wet grass. The wall behind him – his only point of anchorage in this wasteland – became a ghost of itself, then faded entirely. Committed now, he walked on a few more steps, not certain that he was even taking a straight route. Suddenly the fog curtain was drawn aside and he saw a figure waiting for him a few yards ahead. The bruises now twisted his face so badly Ballard would not have known it to be Mironenko, but that his eyes still burned so brightly.

The man did not wait for Ballard, but turned again and loped off into insolidity, leaving the Englishman to follow, cursing both the chase and the quarry. As he did so, he felt a movement close by. His senses were useless in the clammy embrace of fog and night, but he saw with that other eye, heard with that other ear, and he knew he was not alone. Had Mironenko given up the race and come back to escort him? He spoke the man's name, knowing that in doing so he made his position apparent to any and all, but equally certain that whoever stalked him already knew precisely where he stood.

'Speak,' he said.

There was no reply out of the fog.

Then; movement. The fog curled upon itself and Ballard glimpsed a form dividing the veils. Mironenko! He called after the man again, taking several steps through the murk in pursuit and suddenly something was stepping out to meet him. He saw the phantom for a moment only; long enough to glimpse incandescent eyes and teeth grown so vast they wrenched the mouth into a permanent grimace. Of those facts – eyes and teeth – he was certain. Of the other bizarrities – the bristling flesh, the monstrous limbs – he was less sure. Maybe his mind, exhausted with so much noise and pain, was finally losing its grip on the real world; inventing terrors to frighten him back into ignorance.

'Damn you,' he said, defying both the thunder that was coming to blind him again and the phantoms he would be blinded to. Almost as if to test his defiance, the fog up ahead shimmered and parted and something that he might have taken for human, but that it had its belly to the ground, slunk into view and out. To his right, he heard growls; to his left, another indeterminate form came and went. He was surrounded, it seemed, by mad men and wild dogs.

And Mironenko; where was he? Part of this assembly, or prey to it? Hearing a half-word spoken behind him, he swung round to see a figure that was plausibly that of the Russian backing into the fog. This time he didn't walk in pursuit, he *ran*, and his speed was rewarded. The figure reappeared ahead of him, and Ballard stretched to snatch at the man's jacket. His fingers found purchase, and all at once Mironenko was reeling round, a growl in his throat, and Ballard was staring into a face that almost made him cry out. His mouth was a raw wound, the teeth vast, the eyes slits of molten gold; the lumps at his neck had swelled and spread, so that the Russian's head was no longer raised above his body but part of one undivided energy, head becoming torso without an axis intervening.

'Ballard,' the beast smiled.

Its voice clung to coherence only with the greatest difficulty, but Ballard heard the remnants of Mironenko there. The more he scanned the simmering flesh, the more appalled he became.

'Don't be afraid,' Mironenko said.

'What disease is this?'

'The only disease I ever suffered was forgetfulness, and I'm cured of that –' He grimaced as he spoke, as if each word was shaped in contradiction to the instincts of his throat.

Ballard touched his hand to his head. Despite his revolt against the pain, the noise was rising and rising.

'. . . You remember too, don't you? You're the same.'

'No,' Ballard muttered.

Mironenko reached a spine-haired palm to touch him. 'Don't be afraid,' he said. 'You're not alone. There are many of us. Brothers and sisters.'

'I'm not your brother,' Ballard said. The noise was bad, but the face of Mironenko was worse. Revolted, he turned his back on it, but the Russian only followed him.

'Don't you taste freedom, Ballard? And life. Just a breath away.' Ballard walked on, the blood beginning to creep from his nostrils. He let it come. 'It only hurts for a while,' Mironenko said. 'Then the pain goes . . .'

Ballard kept his head down, eyes to the earth. Mironenko, seeing that he was making little impression, dropped behind.

'They won't take you back!' he said. 'You've seen too much.'

The roar of helicopters did not entirely blot these words out. Ballard knew there was truth in them. His step faltered, and through the cacophony he heard Mironenko murmur:

'Look . . .'

Ahead, the fog had thinned somewhat, and the park wall was visible through rags of mist. Behind him, Mironenko's voice had descended to a snarl.

'*Look at what you are.*'

The rotors roared; Ballard's legs felt as though they would fold up beneath him. But he kept up his advance towards the wall. Within yards of it, Mironenko called after him again, but this time the words had fled altogether. There was only a low growl. Ballard could not resist looking; just once. He glanced over his shoulder.

Again the fog confounded him, but not entirely. For moments that were both an age and yet too brief, Ballard saw the thing that had been Mironenko in all its glory, and at the sight the rotors grew to screaming pitch. He clamped his hands to his face. As he did so a shot rang out; then another; then a volley of shots. He fell to the ground, as much in weakness as in self-defence, and uncovered his eyes to see several human figures moving in the fog. Though he had forgotten their pursuers, they had not forgotten him. They had traced him to the park, and stepped into the midst of this lunacy, and now men and half-men and things not men were lost in the fog, and there was bloody confusion on every side. He saw a gunman firing at a shadow, only to have an ally appear from the fog with a bullet in his belly; saw a thing appear on four legs and flit from sight again on two; saw another run by carrying a human head by the hair, and laughing from its snouted face.

The turmoil spilled towards him. Fearing for his life, he stood up and staggered back towards the wall. The cries and shots and snarls went on; he expected either bullet or beast to find him with every step. But he reached the wall alive, and attempted to scale it. His co-ordination had deserted him, however. He had no choice but to follow the wall along its length until he reached the gate.

Behind him the scenes of unmasking and transformation and mistaken identity went on. His enfeebled thoughts turned briefly to Mironenko. Would he, or any of his tribe, survive this massacre?

'Ballard,' said a voice in the fog. He couldn't see the speaker, although he recognised the voice. He'd heard it in his delusion, and it had told him lies.

He felt a pin-prick at his neck. The man had come from behind, and was pressing a needle into him.

'Sleep,' the voice said. And with the words came oblivion.

At first he couldn't remember the man's name. His mind wandered like a lost child, although his interrogator would time and again demand his attention, speaking to him as though they were old friends. And there was indeed something familiar about his errant eye, that went on its way so much more slowly than its companion. At last, the name came to him.

'You're Cripps,' he said.

'Of course I'm Cripps,' the man replied. 'Is your memory playing tricks? Don't concern yourself. I've given you some suppressants, to keep you from losing your balance. Not that I think that's very likely. You've fought the good fight, Ballard, in spite of considerable provocation. When I think of the way Odell snapped . . .' He sighed. 'Do you remember last night at all?'

At first his mind's eye was blind. But then the memories began to come. Vague forms moving in a fog.

'The park,' he said at last.

'I only just got you out. God knows how many are dead.'

'The other . . . the Russian . . .?'

'Mironenko?' Cripps prompted. 'I don't know. I'm not in charge any longer, you see; I just stepped in to salvage something if I could. London will need us again, sooner or later. Especially now they know the Russians have a special corps like us. We'd heard rumours of course; and then, after you'd met with him, began to wonder about Mironenko. That's why I set up the meeting. And of course when I saw him, face to face, I *knew*. There's something in the eyes. Something hungry.'

'I saw him change –'

'Yes, it's quite a sight, isn't it? The power it unleashes. That's why we developed the programme, you see, to harness that power, to have it work for us. But it's difficult to control. It took years of suppression therapy, slowly burying the desire for transformation, so that what we had left was a man with a beast's faculties. A wolf in sheep's clothing. We thought we had the problem beaten; that if the belief systems didn't keep you subdued the pain response would. But we were wrong.' He stood up and crossed to the window. 'Now we have to start again.'

'Suckling said you'd been wounded.'

'No. Merely demoted. Ordered back to London.'

'But you're not going.'

'I will now; now that I've found you.' He looked round at Ballard. 'You're my vindication, Ballard. You're living proof that my techniques are viable. You have full knowledge of your condition, yet the therapy holds the leash.' He turned back to the window. Rain lashed the glass. Ballard could almost feel it upon his head, upon his back. Cool, sweet rain. For a blissful moment he seemed to be running in it, close to the ground, and the air was full of the scents the downpour had released from the pavements.

'Mironenko said –'

'Forget Mironenko,' Cripps told him. 'He's dead. You're the last of the old order, Ballard. And the first of the new.'

Downstairs, a bell rang. Cripps peered out of the window at the streets below.

'Well, well,' he said. 'A delegation, come to beg us to return. I hope you're flattered.' He went to the door. 'Stay here. We needn't show you off tonight. You're weary. Let them wait, eh? Let them sweat.' He left the stale room, closing the door behind him. Ballard heard his footsteps on the stairs. The bell was being rung a second time. He got up and crossed to the window. The weariness of the late afternoon light matched his weariness; he and his city were still of one accord, despite the curse that was upon him. Below a man emerged from the back of the car and crossed to the front door. Even at this acute angle Ballard recognised Suckling.

There were voices in the hallway; and with Suckling's appearance the debate seemed to become more heated. Ballard went to the door, and listened, but his drug-dulled mind could make little sense of the argument. He prayed that Cripps would keep to his word, and not allow them to peer at him. He didn't want to be a beast like Mironenko. It wasn't freedom, was it, to be so terrible? It was merely a different kind of tyranny. But then he didn't want to be the first of Cripps' heroic new order either. He belonged to nobody, he realised; not even himself. He was hopelessly lost. And yet hadn't Mironenko said at that first meeting that the man who did not believe himself lost, *was* lost? Perhaps better that – better to exist in the twilight between one state

128

and another, to prosper as best he could by doubt and ambiguity – than to suffer the certainties of the tower.

The debate below was gaining in momentum. Ballard opened the door so as to hear better. It was Suckling's voice that met him. The tone was waspish, but no less threatening for that.

'It's over . . .' he was telling Cripps '. . . don't you understand plain English?' Cripps made an attempt to protest, but Suckling cut him short. 'Either you come in a gentlemanly fashion or Gideon and Sheppard carry you out. Which is it to be?'

'What is this?' Cripps demanded. 'You're nobody, Suckling. You're comic relief.'

'That was yesterday,' the man replied. 'There've been some changes made. Every dog has his day, isn't that right? You should know that better than anybody. I'd get a coat if I were you. It's raining.'

There was a short silence, then Cripps said:

'All right. I'll come.'

'Good man,' said Suckling sweetly. 'Gideon, go check upstairs.'

'I'm alone,' said Cripps.

'I believe you,' said Suckling. Then to Gideon, 'Do it anyway.'

Ballard heard somebody move across the hallway, and then a sudden flurry of movement. Cripps was either making an escape-bid or attacking Suckling, one of the two. Suckling shouted out; there was a scuffle. Then, cutting through the confusion, a single shot.

Cripps cried out, then came the sound of him falling.

Now Suckling's voice, thick with fury. 'Stupid,' he said. 'Stupid.'

Cripps groaned something which Ballard didn't catch. Had he asked to be dispatched, perhaps, for Suckling

129

told him: 'No. You're going back to London. Sheppard, stop him bleeding. Gideon; upstairs.'

Ballard backed away from the head of the stairs as Gideon began his ascent. He felt sluggish and inept. There was no way out of this trap. They would corner him and exterminate him. He was a beast; a mad dog in a maze. If he'd only killed Suckling when he'd had the strength to do so. But then what good would that have done? The world was full of men like Suckling, men biding their time until they could show their true colours; vile, soft, secret men. And suddenly the beast seemed to move in Ballard, and he thought of the park and the fog and the smile on the face of Mironenko, and he felt a surge of grief for something he'd never had: the life of a monster.

Gideon was almost at the top of the stairs. Though it could only delay the inevitable by moments, Ballard slipped along the landing and opened the first door he found. It was the bathroom. There was a bolt on the door, which he slipped into place.

The sound of running water filled the room. A piece of guttering had broken, and was delivering a torrent of rain-water onto the window-sill. The sound, and the chill of the bathroom, brought the night of delusions back. He remembered the pain and blood; remembered the shower – water beating on his skull, cleansing him of the taming pain. At the thought, four words came to his lips unbidden.

'I do not believe.'

He had been heard.

'There's somebody up here,' Gideon called. The man approached the door, and beat on it. 'Open up!'

Ballard heard him quite clearly, but didn't reply. His throat was burning, and the roar of rotors was growing louder again. He put his back to the door and despaired.

Suckling was up the stairs and at the door in seconds. 'Who's in there?' he demanded to know. 'Answer me! Who's in *there?*' Getting no response, he ordered that Cripps be brought upstairs. There was more commotion as the order was obeyed.

'For the last time –' Suckling said.

The pressure was building in Ballard's skull. This time it seemed the din had lethal intentions; his eyes ached, as if about to be blown from their sockets. He caught sight of something in the mirror above the sink; something with gleaming eyes, and again, the words came – 'I do not believe' – but this time his throat, hot with other business, could barely pronounce them.

'*Ballard*,' said Suckling. There was triumph in the word. 'My God, we've got Ballard as well. This is our lucky day.'

No, thought the man in the mirror. There was nobody of that name here. Nobody of any name at all, in fact, for weren't names the first act of faith, the first board in the box you buried freedom in? The thing he was becoming would not be named; nor boxed; nor buried. Never again.

For a moment he lost sight of the bathroom, and found himself hovering above the grave they had made him dig, and in the depths the box danced as its contents fought its premature burial. He could hear the wood splintering – or was it the sound of the door being broken down?

The box-lid flew off. A rain of nails fell on the heads of the burial party. The noise in his head, as if knowing that its torments had proved fruitless, suddenly fled, and with it the delusion. He was back in the bathroom, facing the open door. The men who stared through at him had the faces of fools. Slack, and stupefied with shock – seeing the way he was wrought. Seeing the snout of him, the hair of him, the golden eye and the yellow tooth of him. Their horror elated him.

'Kill it!' said Suckling, and pushed Gideon into the breach. The man already had his gun from his pocket and was levelling it, but his trigger-finger was too slow. The beast snatched his hand and pulped the flesh around the steel. Gideon screamed, and stumbled away down the stairs, ignoring Suckling's shouts.

As the beast raised his hand to sniff the blood on his palm there was a flash of fire, and he felt the blow to his shoulder. Sheppard had no chance to fire a second shot however before his prey was through the door and upon him. Forsaking his gun, he made a futile bid for the stairs, but the beast's hand unsealed the back of his head in one easy stroke. The gunman toppled forward, the narrow landing filling with the smell of him. Forgetting his other enemies, the beast fell upon the offal and ate.

Somebody said: 'Ballard.'

The beast swallowed down the dead man's eyes in one gulp, like prime oysters.

Again, those syllables. '*Ballard*.' He would have gone on with his meal, but that the sound of weeping pricked his ears. Dead to himself he was, but not to grief. He dropped the meat from his fingers and looked back along the landing.

The man who was crying only wept from one eye; the other gazed on, oddly untouched. But the pain in the living eye was profound indeed. It was *despair*, the beast knew; such suffering was too close to him for the sweetness of transformation to have erased it entirely. The weeping man was locked in the arms of another man, who had his gun placed against the side of his prisoner's head.

'If you make another move,' the captor said, 'I'll blow his head off. Do you understand me?'

The beast wiped his mouth.

'Tell him, Cripps! He's your baby. Make him understand.'

The one-eyed man tried to speak, but words defeated him. Blood from the wound in his abdomen seeped between his fingers.

'Neither of you need die,' the captor said. The beast didn't like the music of his voice; it was shrill and deceitful. 'London would much prefer to have you alive. So why don't you tell him, Cripps? Tell him I mean him no harm.'

The weeping man nodded.

'Ballard . . .' he murmured. His voice was softer than the other. The beast listened.

'Tell me, Ballard –' he said, '– how does it feel?'

The beast couldn't quite make sense of the question.

'Please tell me. For curiosity's sake –'

'Damn you –' said Suckling, pressing the gun into Cripps' flesh. 'This isn't a debating society.'

'Is it good?' Cripps asked, ignoring both man and gun.

'Shut up!'

'Answer me, Ballard. *How does it feel?*'

As he stared into Cripps' despairing eyes the meaning of the sounds he'd uttered came clear, the words falling into place like the pieces of a mosaic. 'Is it good?' the man was asking.

Ballard heard laughter in his throat, and found the syllables there to reply.

'Yes,' he told the weeping man. 'Yes. It's good.'

He had not finished his reply before Cripps' hand sped to snatch at Suckling's. Whether he intended suicide or escape nobody would ever know. The trigger-finger twitched, and a bullet flew up through Cripps' head and spread his despair across the ceiling. Suckling threw the body off, and went to level the gun, but the beast was already upon him.

Had he been more of a man, Ballard might have thought to make Suckling suffer, but he had no such perverse ambition. His only thought was to render the enemy extinct as efficiently as possible. Two sharp and lethal blows did it. Once the man was dispatched, Ballard crossed over to where Cripps was lying. His glass eye had escaped destruction. It gazed on fixedly, untouched by the holocaust all around them. Unseating it from the maimed head, Ballard put in his pocket; then he went out into the rain.

It was dusk. He did not know which district of Berlin he'd been brought to, but his impulses, freed of reason, led him via the back streets and shadows to a wasteland on the outskirts of the city, in the middle of which stood a solitary ruin. It was anybody's guess as to what the building might once have been (an abbatoir? an opera-house?) but by some freak of fate it had escaped demolition, though every other building had been levelled for several hundred yards in each direction. As he made his way across the weed-clogged rubble the wind changed direction by a few degrees and carried the scent of his tribe to him. There were many there, together in the shelter of the ruin. Some leaned their backs against the wall and shared a cigarette; some were perfect wolves, and haunted the darkness like ghosts with golden eyes; yet others might have passed for human entirely, but for their trails.

Though he feared that names would be forbidden amongst this clan, he asked two lovers who were rutting in the shelter of the wall if they knew of a man called Mironenko. The bitch had a smooth and hairless back, and a dozen full teats hanging from her belly.

'Listen,' she said.

Ballard listened, and heard somebody talking in a corner of the ruin. The voice ebbed and flowed. He followed the sound across the roofless interior to where a wolf was standing, surrounded by an attentive audience, an open book in its front paws. At Ballard's approach one or two of the audience turned their luminous eyes up to him. The reader halted.

'Ssh!' said one, 'the Comrade is reading to us.'

It was Mironenko who spoke. Ballard slipped into the ring of listeners beside him, as the reader took up the story afresh.

'*And God blessed them, and God said unto them, Be fruitful, and multiply, and replenish the earth . . .*'

Ballard had heard the words before, but tonight they were new.

'*. . . and subdue it: and have dominion over the fish of the sea, and over the fowl of the air . . .*'

He looked around the circle of listeners as the words described their familiar pattern.

'*. . . and over every living thing that moveth upon the earth.*'

Somewhere near, a beast was crying.

THE LAST ILLUSION

WHAT HAPPENED THEN – when the magician, having mesmerised the caged tiger, pulled the tasselled cord that released a dozen swords upon its head – was the subject of heated argument both in the bar of the theatre and later, when Swann's performance was over, on the sidewalk of 51st Street. Some claimed to have glimpsed the bottom of the cage opening in the split second that all other eyes were on the descending blades, and seen the tiger swiftly spirited away as the woman in the red dress took its place behind the lacquered bars. Others were just as adamant that the animal had never been in the cage to begin with, its presence merely a projection which had been extinguished as a mechanism propelled the woman from beneath the stage; this, of course, at such a speed that it deceived the eye of all but those swift and suspicious enough to catch it. And the swords? The nature of the trick which had transformed them in the mere seconds of their gleaming descent from steel to rose-petals was yet further fuel for debate. The explanations ranged from the prosaic to the elaborate, but few of the throng that left the theatre lacked some theory. Nor did the arguments finish there, on the sidewalk. They raged on, no doubt, in the apartments and restaurants of New York.

The pleasure to be had from Swann's illusions was, it seemed, twofold. First: the spectacle of the trick itself – in the breathless moment when disbelief was, if not suspended, at least taken on tip-toe. And second, when the moment was over and logic restored, in the debate as to how the trick had been achieved.

'How do you do it, Mr Swann?' Barbara Bernstein was eager to know.

'It's magic,' Swann replied. He had invited her backstage to examine the tiger's cage for any sign of fakery in its construction; she had found none. She had examined the swords: they were lethal. And the petals, fragrant. Still she insisted:

'Yes, but *really* . . .' she leaned close to him. 'You can tell me,' she said, 'I promise I won't breathe a word to a soul.'

He returned her a slow smile in place of a reply.

'Oh, I know . . .' she said, 'you're going to tell me that you've signed some kind of oath.'

'That's right,' Swann said.

'– And you're forbidden to give away any trade secrets.'

'The intention is to give you pleasure,' he told her. 'Have I failed in that?'

'Oh no,' she replied, without a moment's hesitation. 'Everybody's talking about the show. You're the toast of New York.'

'No,' he protested.

'Truly,' she said, 'I know people who would give their eye-teeth to get into this theatre. And to have a guided tour backstage . . . well, I'll be the envy of everybody.'

'I'm pleased,' he said, and touched her face. She had clearly been anticipating such a move on his part. It would be something else for her to boast of: her seduction by the man critics had dubbed the Magus of Manhattan.

'I'd like to make love to you,' he whispered to her.

'Here?' she said.

'No,' he told her. 'Not within ear-shot of the tigers.'

She laughed. She preferred her lovers twenty years Swann's junior – he looked, someone had observed, like a man in mourning for his profile, but his touch promised wit no boy could offer. She liked the tang of dissolution she sensed beneath his gentlemanly façade. Swann was a dangerous man. If she turned him down she might never find another.

'We could go to a hotel,' she suggested.

'A hotel,' he said, 'is a good idea.'

A look of doubt had crossed her face.

'What about your wife . . .?' she said. 'We might be seen.'

He took her hand. 'Shall we be invisible, then?'

'I'm serious.'

'So am I,' he insisted. 'Take it from me; seeing is not believing. I should know. It's the cornerstone of my profession.' She did not look much reassured. 'If anyone recognises us,' he told her, 'I'll simply tell them their eyes are playing tricks.'

She smiled at this, and he kissed her. She returned the kiss with unquestionable fervour.

'Miraculous,' he said, when their mouths parted. 'Shall we go before the tigers gossip?'

He led her across the stage. The cleaners had not yet got about their business, and there, lying on the boards, was a litter of rose-buds. Some had been trampled, a few had not. Swann took his hand from hers, and walked across to where the flowers lay.

She watched him stoop to pluck a rose from the ground, enchanted by the gesture, but before he could stand upright again something in the air above him caught her eye. She looked up and her gaze met a slice of silver that was even now plunging towards him. She made to warn him, but the sword was quicker than her tongue. At the last possible moment he seemed to sense the danger he was in and looked round, the bud in his hand, as the point met his back. The sword's momentum carried it through his body to the hilt. Blood fled from his chest, and splashed the floor. He made no sound, but fell forward, forcing two-thirds of the sword's length out of his body again as he hit the stage.

She would have screamed, but that her attention was claimed by a sound from the clutter of magical apparatus arrayed in the wings behind her, a muttered growl which was indisputably the voice of the tiger. She froze. There were probably instructions on how best to stare down rogue tigers, but as a Manhattanite born and bred they were techniques she wasn't acquainted with.

'Swann?' she said, hoping this yet might be some baroque illusion staged purely for her benefit. 'Swann. Please get up.'

But the magician only lay where he had fallen, the pool spreading from beneath him.

'If this is a joke –' she said testily, '– I'm not amused.' When he didn't rise to her remark she tried a sweeter tactic. 'Swann, my sweet, I'd like to go now, if you don't mind.'

The growl came again. She didn't want to turn and seek out its source, but equally she didn't want to be sprung upon from behind.

Cautiously she looked round. The wings were in darkness. The clutter of properties kept her from working out the precise location of the beast. She could hear it still, however: its tread, its growl. Step by step, she retreated towards the apron of the stage. The closed curtains sealed her off from the auditorium, but she hoped she might scramble under them before the tiger reached her.

As she backed against the heavy fabric, one of the shadows in the wings forsook its ambiguity, and the animal appeared. It was not beautiful, as she had thought it when behind bars. It was vast and lethal and hungry. She went down on her haunches and reached for the hem of the curtain. The fabric was heavily weighted, and she had more difficulty lifting it than she'd expected, but she had managed to slide halfway under the drape when, head and hands pressed to the boards, she sensed the thump of the tiger's advance. An instant later she felt the splash of its breath on her bare back, and screamed as it hooked its talons into her body and hauled her from the sight of safety towards its steaming jaws.

Even then, she refused to give up her life. She kicked at it, and tore out its fur in handfuls, and delivered a hail of punches to its snout. But her resistance was negligible in the face of such authority; her assault, for all its ferocity, did not slow the beast a jot. It ripped open her body with one casual clout. Mercifully, with that first wound her senses gave up all claim to verisimilitude, and took instead to preposterous invention. It seemed to her that she heard applause from somewhere, and the roar of an approving audience, and that in place

140

of the blood that was surely springing from her body there came fountains of sparkling light. The agony her nerve-endings were suffering didn't touch her at all. Even when the animal had divided her into three or four parts her head lay on its side at the edge of the stage and watched as her torso was mauled and her limbs devoured.

And all the while, when she wondered how all this could be possible – that her eyes could live to witness this last supper – the only reply she could think of was Swann's:

'*It's magic*,' he'd said.

Indeed, she was thinking that very thing, that this must *be* magic, when the tiger ambled across to her head, and swallowed it down in one bite.

Amongst a certain set Harry D'Amour liked to believe he had some small reputation – a coterie which did not, alas, include his ex-wife, his creditors or those anonymous critics who regularly posted dogs' excrement through his office letterbox. But the woman who was on the phone now, her voice so full of grief she might have been crying for half a year, and was about to begin again, *she* knew him for the paragon he was.

'– I need your help, Mr D'Amour; very badly.'

'I'm busy on several cases at the moment,' he told her. 'Maybe you could come to the office?'

'I can't leave the house,' the woman informed him. 'I'll explain everything. Please come.'

He was sorely tempted. But there *were* several outstanding cases, one of which, if not solved soon, might end in fratricide. He suggested she try elsewhere.

'I can't go to just anybody,' the woman insisted.

'Why me?'

'I read about you. About what happened in Brooklyn.'

Making mention of his most conspicuous failure was not the surest method of securing his services, Harry thought, but it certainly got his attention. What had happened in Wyckoff Street had begun innocently enough, with a husband who'd employed him to spy on his adulterous wife, and had ended on the top storey of the Lomax house with the world he thought he'd known turning inside out. When the body-count was done, and the surviving priests dispatched, he was left with a fear of stairs, and more questions than he'd ever answer this side of the family plot. He took no pleasure in being reminded of those terrors.

'I don't like to talk about Brooklyn,' he said.

'Forgive me,' the woman replied, 'but I need somebody who has experience with . . . with the occult.' She stopped speaking for a moment. He could still hear her breath down the line: soft, but erratic.

'I need you,' she said. He had already decided, in that pause when only her fear had been audible, what reply he would make.

'I'll come.'

'I'm grateful to you,' she said. 'The house is on East 61st Street –' He scribbled down the details. Her last words were, 'Please hurry.' Then she put down the phone.

He made some calls, in the vain hope of placating two of his more excitable clients, then pulled on his jacket, locked the office, and started downstairs. The landing and the lobby smelt pungent. As he reached the front door he caught Chaplin, the janitor, emerging from the basement.

'This place stinks,' he told the man.

'It's disinfectant.'

'It's cat's piss,' Harry said. 'Get something done about it, will you? I've got a reputation to protect.'

He left the man laughing.

The brownstone on East 61st Street was in pristine condition. He stood on the scrubbed step, sweaty and sour-breathed, and felt like a slob. The expression on the face that met him when the door opened did nothing to dissuade him of that opinion.

'Yes?' it wanted to know.

'I'm Harry D'Amour,' he said. 'I got a call.'

The man nodded. 'You'd better come in,' he said without enthusiasm.

It was cooler in than out; and sweeter. The place reeked of perfume. Harry followed the disapproving face down the hallway and into a large room, on the other side of which – across an oriental carpet that had everything woven into its pattern but the price – sat a widow. She didn't suit black; nor tears. She stood up and offered her hand.

'Mr D'Amour?'

'Yes.'

'Valentin will get you something to drink if you'd like.'

'Please. Milk, if you have it.' His belly had been jittering for the last hour; since her talk of Wyckoff Street, in fact.

Valentin retired from the room, not taking his beady eyes off Harry until the last possible moment.

'Somebody died,' said Harry, once the man had gone.

'That's right,' the widow said, sitting down again. At her invitation he sat opposite her, amongst enough cushions to furnish a harem. 'My husband.'

'I'm sorry.'

'There's no time to be sorry,' she said, her every look and gesture betraying her words. He was glad of her

143

grief; the tearstains and the fatigue blemished a beauty which, had he seen it unimpaired, might have rendered him dumb with admiration.

'They say that my husband's death was an accident,' she was saying. 'I know it wasn't.'

'May I ask . . . your name?'

'I'm sorry. My name is Swann, Mr D'Amour. Dorothea Swann. You may have heard of my husband?'

'The magician?'

'*Illusionist*,' she said.

'I read about it. Tragic.'

'Did you ever see his performance?'

Harry shook his head. 'I can't afford Broadway, Mrs Swann.'

'We were only over for three months, while his show ran. We were going back in September . . .'

'Back?'

'To Hamburg,' she said. 'I don't like this city. It's too hot. And too cruel.'

'Don't blame New York,' he said. 'It can't help itself.'

'Maybe,' she replied, nodding. 'Perhaps what happened to Swann would have happened anyway, wherever we'd been. People keep telling me: it was an accident. That's all. Just an accident.'

'But you don't believe it?'

Valentin had appeared with a glass of milk. He set it down on the table in front of Harry. As he made to leave, she said: 'Valentin. The letter?'

He looked at her strangely, almost as though she'd said something obscene.

'*The letter*,' she repeated.

He exited.

'You were saying –'

She frowned. 'What?'

144

'About it being an accident.'

'Oh yes. I lived with Swann seven and a half years, and I got to understand him as well as anybody ever could. I learned to sense when he wanted me around, and when he didn't. When he didn't, I'd take myself off somewhere and let him have his privacy. Genius needs privacy. And he *was* a genius, you know. The greatest illusionist since Houdini.'

'Is that so?'

'I'd think sometimes – it was a kind of miracle that he let me into his life . . .'

Harry wanted to say Swann would have been mad not to have done so, but the comment was inappropriate. She didn't want blandishments; didn't need them. Didn't need anything, perhaps, but her husband alive again.

'Now I think I didn't know him at all,' she went on, 'didn't *understand* him. I think maybe it was another trick. Another part of his magic.'

'I called him a magician a while back,' Harry said. 'You corrected me.'

'So I did,' she said, conceding his point with an apologetic look. 'Forgive me. That was Swann talking. He *hated* to be called a magician. He said that was a word that had to be kept for miracle-workers.'

'And he was no miracle-worker?'

'He used to call himself the Great Pretender,' she said. The thought made her smile.

Valentin had re-appeared, his lugubrious features rife with suspicion. He carried an envelope, which he clearly had no desire to give up. Dorothea had to cross the carpet and take it from his hands.

'Is this wise?' he said.

'Yes,' she told him.

He turned on his heel and made a smart withdrawal.

'He's grief-stricken,' she said. 'Forgive him his behaviour. He was with Swann from the beginning of his career. I think he loved my husband as much as I did.'

She ran her finger down into the envelope and pulled the letter out. The paper was pale yellow, and gossamer-thin.

'A few hours after he died, this letter was delivered here by hand,' she said. 'It was addressed to him. I opened it. I think you ought to read it.'

She passed it to him. The hand it was written in was solid and unaffected.

Dorothea, he had written, *if you are reading this, then I am dead.*

You know how little store I set by dreams and premonitions and such; but for the last few days strange thoughts have just crept into my head, and I have the suspicion that death is very close to me. If so, so. There's no help for it. Don't waste time trying to puzzle out the whys and wherefores; they're old news now. Just know that I love you, and that I have always loved you in my way. I'm sorry for whatever unhappiness I've caused, or am causing now, but it was out of my hands.

I have some instructions regarding the disposal of my body. Please adhere to them to the letter. Don't let anybody try to persuade you out of doing as I ask.

I want you to have my body watched night and day *until I'm cremated. Don't try and take my remains back to Europe. Have me cremated here,* as soon as possible, *then throw the ashes in the East River.*

My sweet darling, I'm afraid. Not of bad dreams, or of what might happen to me in this life, but of what my enemies may try to do once I'm dead. You know how critics can be: they wait until you can't fight them back, then they start the character assassinations. It's too long a business to try and explain all of this, so I must simply trust you to do as I say.

Again, I love you, and I hope you never have to read this letter.

Your adoring,

Swann.'

'Some farewell note,' Harry commented when he'd read it through twice. He folded it up and passed it back to the widow.

'I'd like you to stay with him,' she said. 'Corpse-sit, if you will. Just until all the legal formalities are dealt with and I can make arrangements for his cremation. It shouldn't take them long. I've got a lawyer working on it now.'

'Again: why me?'

She avoided his gaze. 'As he says in the letter, he was never superstitious. But I am. I believe in omens. And there was an odd atmosphere about the place in the days before he died. As if we were watched.'

'You think he was murdered?'

She mused on this, then said: 'I don't believe it was an accident.'

'These enemies he talks about . . .'

'He was a great man. Much envied.'

'Professional jealousy? Is that a motive for murder?'

'Anything can be a motive, can't it?' she said. 'People get killed for the colour of their eyes, don't they?'

Harry was impressed. It had taken him twenty years to learn how arbitrary things were. She spoke it as conventional wisdom.

'Where is your husband?' he asked her.

'Upstairs,' she said. 'I had the body brought back here, where I could look after him. I can't pretend I understand what's going on, but I'm not going to risk ignoring his instructions.'

Harry nodded.

147

'Swann was my life,' she added softly, apropos of nothing; and everything.

She took him upstairs. The perfume that had met him at the door intensified. The master bedroom had been turned into a Chapel of Rest, knee-deep in sprays and wreaths of every shape and variety; their mingled scents verged on the hallucinogenic. In the midst of this abundance, the casket – an elaborate affair in black and silver – was mounted on trestles. The upper half of the lid stood open, the plush overlay folded back. At Dorothea's invitation he waded through the tributes to view the deceased. He liked Swann's face; it had humour, and a certain guile; it was even handsome in its weary way. More: it had inspired the love of Dorothea; a face could have few better recommendations. Harry stood waist-high in flowers and, absurd as it was, felt a twinge of envy for the love this man must have enjoyed.

'Will you help me, Mr D'Amour?'

What could he say but: 'Yes, of course I'll help.' That, and: 'Call me Harry.'

He would be missed at Wing's Pavilion tonight. He had occupied the best table there every Friday night for the past six and a half years, eating at one sitting enough to compensate for what his diet lacked in excellence and variety the other six days of the week. This feast – the best Chinese cuisine to be had south of Canal Street – came *gratis*, thanks to services he had once rendered the owner. Tonight the table would go empty.

Not that his stomach suffered. He had only been sitting with Swann an hour or so when Valentin came up and said:

'How do you like your steak?'

148

'Just shy of burned,' Harry replied.

Valentin was none too pleased by the response. 'I hate to overcook good steak,' he said.

'And I hate the sight of blood,' Harry said, 'even if it isn't my own.'

The chef clearly despaired of his guest's palate, and turned to go.

'Valentin?'

The man looked round.

'Is that your Christian name?' Harry asked.

'Christian names are for Christians,' came the reply.

Harry nodded. 'You don't like my being here, am I right?'

Valentin made no reply. His eyes had drifted past Harry to the open coffin.

'I'm not going to be here for long,' Harry said, 'but while I am, can't we be friends?'

Valentin's gaze found him once more.

'I don't have any friends,' he said without enmity or self-pity. 'Not now.'

'OK. I'm sorry.'

'What's to be sorry for?' Valentin wanted to know. 'Swann's dead. It's all over, bar the shouting.'

The doleful face stoically refused tears. A stone would weep sooner, Harry guessed. But there was grief there, and all the more acute for being dumb.

'One question.'

'Only one?'

'Why didn't you want me to read his letter?'

Valentin raised his eyebrows slightly; they were fine enough to have been pencilled on. 'He wasn't insane,' he said. 'I didn't want you thinking he was a crazy man, because of what he wrote. What you read you keep to yourself. Swann was a legend. I don't want his memory besmirched.'

149

'You should write a book,' Harry said. 'Tell the whole story once and for all. You were with him a long time, I hear.'

'Oh yes,' said Valentin. 'Long enough to know better than to tell the truth.'

So saying he made an exit, leaving the flowers to wilt, and Harry with more puzzles on his hands than he'd begun with.

Twenty minutes later, Valentin brought up a tray of food: a large salad, bread, wine, and the steak. It was one degree short of charcoal.

'Just the way I like it,' Harry said, and set to guzzling.

He didn't see Dorothea Swann, though God knows he thought about her often enough. Every time he heard a whisper on the stairs, or footsteps along the carpetted landing, he hoped her face would appear at the door, an invitation on her lips. Not perhaps the most appropriate of thoughts, given the proximity of her husband's corpse, but what would the illusionist care now? He was dead and gone. If he had any generosity of spirit he wouldn't want to see his widow drown in her grief.

Harry drank the half-carafe of wine Valentin had brought, and when – three-quarters of an hour later – the man re-appeared with coffee and Calvados, he told him to leave the bottle.

Nightfall was near. The traffic was noisy on Lexington and Third. Out of boredom he took to watching the street from the window. Two lovers feuded loudly on the sidewalk, and only stopped when a brunette with a hare-lip and a pekinese stood watching them shamelessly. There were preparations for a party in the brownstone opposite: he watched a table lovingly laid, and candles lit. After a time the spying began to

150

depress him, so he called Valentin and asked if there was a portable television he could have access to. No sooner said than provided, and for the next two hours he sat with the small black and white monitor on the floor amongst the orchids and the lilies, watching whatever mindless entertainment it offered, the silver luminescence flickering on the blooms like excitable moonlight.

A quarter after midnight, with the party across the street in full swing, Valentin came up. 'You want a night-cap?' he asked.

'Sure.'

'Milk; or something stronger?'

'Something stronger.'

He produced a bottle of fine cognac, and two glasses. Together they toasted the dead man.

'Mr Swann.'

'Mr Swann.'

'If you need anything more tonight,' Valentin said, 'I'm in the room directly above. Mrs Swann is down-stairs, so if you hear somebody moving about, don't worry. She doesn't sleep well these nights.'

'Who does?' Harry replied.

Valentin left him to his vigil. Harry heard the man's tread on the stairs, and then the creaking of floorboards on the level above. He returned his attention to the television, but he'd lost the thread of the movie he'd been watching. It was a long stretch 'til dawn; meanwhile New York would be having itself a fine Friday night: dancing, fighting, fooling around.

The picture on the television set began to flicker. He stood up, and started to walk across to the set, but he never got there. Two steps from the chair where he'd been sitting the picture folded up and went out altogether, plunging the room into total darkness. Harry briefly had time to register that no light was finding its way through the windows from the street. Then the insanity began.

Something moved in the blackness: vague forms rose and fell. It took him a moment to recognise them. The flowers! Invisible hands were tearing the wreaths and tributes apart, and tossing the blossoms up into the air. He followed their descent, but they didn't hit the ground. It seemed the floorboards had lost all faith in themselves, and disappeared, so the blossoms just kept falling – *down, down* – through the floor of the room below, and through the basement floor, away to God alone knew what destination. Fear gripped Harry, like some old dope-pusher promising a terrible high. Even those few boards that remained beneath his feet were becoming insubstantial. In seconds he would go the way of the blossoms.

He reeled around to locate the chair he'd got up from – some fixed point in this vertiginous nightmare. The chair was still there; he could just discern its form in the gloom. With torn blossoms raining down upon him he reached for it, but even as his hand took hold of the arm, the floor beneath the chair gave up the ghost, and now, by a ghastly light that was thrown up from the pit that yawned beneath his feet, Harry saw it tumble away into Hell, turning over and over 'til it was pin-prick small.

Then it was gone; and the flowers were gone, and the walls and the windows and every damn thing was gone but *him*.

Not quite everything. Swann's casket remained, its lid still standing open, its overlay neatly turned back like the sheet on a child's bed. The trestle had gone, as had the floor beneath the trestle. But the casket floated in the dark air for all the world like some morbid illusion, while from the depths a rumbling

152

sound accompanied the trick like the roll of a snare-drum.

Harry felt the last solidity failing beneath him; felt the pit call. Even as his feet left the ground, that ground faded to nothing, and for a terrifying moment he hung over the Gulfs, his hands seeking the lip of the casket. His right hand caught hold of one of the handles, and closed thankfully around it. His arm was almost jerked from its socket as it took his body-weight, but he flung his other arm up and found the casket-edge. Using it as purchase, he hauled himself up like a half-drowned sailor. It was a strange lifeboat, but then this was a strange sea. Infinitely deep, infinitely terrible.

Even as he laboured to secure himself a better hand-hold, the casket shook, and Harry looked up to discover that the dead man was sitting upright. Swann's eyes opened wide. He turned them on Harry; they were far from benign. The next moment the dead illusionist was scrambling to his feet – the floating casket rocking ever more violently with each movement. Once vertical, Swann proceeded to dislodge his guest by grinding his heel in Harry's knuckles. Harry looked up at Swann, begging for him to stop.

The Great Pretender was a sight to see. His eyes were starting from his sockets; his shirt was torn open to display the exit-wound in his chest. It was bleeding afresh. A rain of cold blood fell upon Harry's upturned face. And still the heel ground at his hands. Harry felt his grip slipping. Swann, sensing his approaching triumph, began to smile.

'Fall, boy!' he said. 'Fall!'

Harry could take no more. In a frenzied effort to save himself he let go of the handle in his right hand, and reached up to snatch at Swann's trouser-leg. His fingers found the hem, and he pulled. The smile vanished from the illusionist's face as he felt his balance go. He reached behind him to take hold of the casket lid for support, but the gesture only tipped the casket further over. The plush cushion tumbled past Harry's head; blossoms followed.

Swann howled in his fury and delivered a vicious kick to Harry's hand. It was an error. The casket tipped over entirely and pitched the man out. Harry had time to glimpse Swann's appalled face as the illusionist fell past him. Then he too lost his grip and tumbled after him.

The dark air whined past his ears. Beneath him, the Gulfs spread their empty arms. And then, behind the rushing in his head, another sound: a human voice.

'Is he dead?' it inquired.

'No,' another voice replied, 'no, I don't think so. What's his name, Dorothea?'

'D'Amour.'

'Mr D'Amour? Mr D'Amour?'

Harry's descent slowed somewhat. Beneath him, the Gulfs roared their rage.

The voice came again, cultivated but unmelodious. 'Mr D'Amour.'

'Harry,' said Dorothea.

At that word, from that voice, he stopped falling; felt himself borne up. He opened his eyes. He was lying on a solid floor, his head inches from the blank television screen. The flowers were all in place around the room, Swann in his casket, and God – if the rumours were to be believed – in his Heaven.

'I'm alive,' he said.

He had quite an audience for his resurrection. Dorothea of course, and two strangers. One, the owner of the voice he'd first heard, stood close to the door. His features were unremarkable, except for his brows and lashes, which were pale to the point of invisibility. His female companion stood nearby. She shared with him this distressing banality, stripped bare of any feature that offered a clue to their natures.

'Help him up, angel,' the man said, and the woman bent to comply. She was stronger than she looked, readily hauling Harry to his feet. He had vomited in his strange sleep. He felt dirty and ridiculous.

'What the hell happened?' he asked, as the woman escorted him to the chair. He sat down.

'He tried to poison you,' the man said.

'Who did?'

'Valentin, of course.'

'Valentin?'

'He's gone,' Dorothea said. 'Just disappeared.' She was shaking. 'I heard you call out, and came in here to find you on the floor. I thought you were going to choke.'

'It's all right,' said the man, 'everything is in order now.'

'Yes,' said Dorothea, clearly reassured by his bland smile. 'This is the lawyer I was telling you about, Harry. Mr Butterfield.'

Harry wiped his mouth. 'Please to meet you,' he said.

'Why don't we all go downstairs?' Butterfield said. 'And I can pay Mr D'Amour what he's due.'

'It's all right,' Harry said, 'I never take my fee until the job's done.'

'But it is done,' Butterfield said. 'Your services are no longer required here.'

Harry threw a glance at Dorothea. She was plucking a withered anthurium from an otherwise healthy spray.

'I was contracted to stay with the body –'

'The arrangements for the disposal of Swann's body have been made,' Butterfield returned. His courtesy was

155

only just intact. 'Isn't that right, Dorothea?'

'It's the middle of the night,' Harry protested. 'You won't get a cremation until tomorrow morning at the earliest.'

'Thank you for your help,' Dorothea said. 'But I'm sure everything will be fine now that Mr Butterfield has arrived. Just fine.'

Butterfield turned to his companion.

'Why don't you go out and find a cab for Mr D'Amour?' he said. Then, looking at Harry: 'We don't want you walking the streets, do we?'

All the way downstairs, and in the hallway as Butterfield paid him off, Harry was willing Dorothea to contradict the lawyer and tell him she wanted Harry to stay. But she didn't even offer him a word of farewell as he was ushered out of the house. The two hundred dollars he'd been given were, of course, more than adequate recompense for the few hours of idleness he'd spent there, but he would happily have burned all the bills for one sign that Dorothea gave a damn that they were parting. Quite clearly she did not. On past experience it would take his bruised ego a full twenty-four hours to recover from such indifference.

He got out of the cab on 3rd around 83rd Street, and walked through to a bar on Lexington where he knew he could put half a bottle of bourbon between himself and the dreams he'd had.

It was well after one. The street was deserted, except for him, and for the echo his footsteps had recently acquired. He turned the corner into Lexington, and waited. A few beats later, Valentin rounded the same corner. Harry took hold of him by his tie.

'Not a bad noose,' he said, hauling the man off his heels.

Valentin made no attempt to free himself. 'Thank God you're alive,' he said.

'No thanks to you,' Harry said. 'What did you put in the drink?'

'Nothing,' Valentin insisted. 'Why should I?'

'So how come I found myself on the floor? How come the bad dreams?'

'Butterfield,' Valentin said. 'Whatever you dreamt, he brought with him, believe me. I panicked as soon as I heard him in the house, I admit it. I know I should have warned you, but I knew if I didn't get out quickly I wouldn't get out at all.'

'Are you telling me he would have killed you?'

'Not personally; but yes.' Harry looked incredulous. 'We go way back, him and me.'

'He's welcome to you,' Harry said, letting go of the tie. 'I'm too damn tired to take any more of this shit.' He turned from Valentin and began to walk away.

'Wait –' said the other man, '– I know I wasn't too sweet with you back at the house, but you've got to understand, things are going to get bad. For both of us.'

'I thought you said it was all over bar the shouting?'

'I thought it was. I thought we had it all sewn up. Then Butterfield arrived and I realised how naïve I was being. They're not going to let Swann rest in peace. Not now, not ever. We have to save him, D'Amour.'

Harry stopped walking and studied the man's face. To pass him in the street, he mused, you wouldn't have taken him for a lunatic.

'Did Butterfield go upstairs?' Valentin enquired.

'Yes he did. Why?'

'Do you remember if he approached the casket?'

Harry shook his head.

'Good,' said Valentin. 'Then the defences are holding,

which gives us a little time. Swann was a fine tactician, you know. But he could be careless. That was how they caught him. Sheer carelessness. He knew they were coming for him. I told him outright, I said we should cancel the remaining performances and go home. At least he had some sanctuary there.'

'You think he was murdered?'

'Jesus Christ,' said Valentin, almost despairing of Harry, 'of course he was murdered.'

'So he's past saving, right? The man's dead.'

'Dead; yes. Past saving? no.'

'Do you talk gibberish to everyone?'

Valentin put his hand on Harry's shoulder, 'Oh no,' he said, with unfeigned sincerity. 'I don't trust anyone the way I trust you.'

'This is very sudden,' said Harry. 'May I ask why?'

'Because you're in this up to your neck, the way I am,' Valentin replied.

'No I'm not,' said Harry, but Valentin ignored the denial, and went on with his talk. 'At the moment we don't know how many of them there are, of course. They might simply have sent Butterfield, but I think that's unlikely.'

'Who's Butterfield with? The Mafia?'

'We should be so lucky,' said Valentin. He reached in his pocket and pulled out a piece of paper. 'This is the woman Swann was with,' he said, 'the night at the theatre. It's possible she knows something of their strength.'

'There was a witness?'

'She didn't come forward, but yes, there was. I was his procurer you see. I helped arrange his several adulteries, so that none ever embarrassed him. See if you can get to her –' He stopped abruptly. Somewhere close by, music was being played. It sounded like a drunken jazz band extemporising on bagpipes; a wheezing, rambling cacophony. Valentin's face instantly became a portrait of distress. 'God help us . . .' he said softly, and began to back away from Harry.

'What's the problem?'

'Do you know how to pray?' Valentin asked him as he retreated down 83rd Street. The volume of the music was rising with every interval.

'I haven't prayed in twenty years,' Harry replied.

'Then *learn*,' came the response, and Valentin turned to run.

As he did so a ripple of darkness moved down the street from the north, dimming the lustre of bar-signs and street-lamps as it came. Neon announcements suddenly guttered and died; there were protests out of upstairs windows as the lights failed and, as if encouraged by the curses, the music took on a fresh and yet more hectic rhythm. Above his head Harry heard a wailing sound, and looked up to see a ragged silhouette against the clouds which trailed tendrils like a man o' war as it descended upon the street, leaving the stench of rotting fish in its wake. Its target was clearly Valentin. He shouted above the wail and the music and the panic from the black-out, but no sooner had he yelled than he heard Valentin shout out from the darkness; a pleading cry that was rudely cut short.

He stood in the murk, his feet unwilling to carry him a step nearer the place from which the plea had come. The smell still stung his nostrils; nosing it, his nausea returned. And then, so did the lights; a wave of power igniting the lamps and the bar-signs as it washed back down the street. It reached Harry, and moved on to the spot where he had last seen Valentin. It was deserted; indeed the sidewalk was empty all the way down to the next intersection.

The drivelling jazz had stopped.

Eyes peeled for man, beast, or the remnants of either, Harry wandered down the sidewalk. Twenty yards from where he had been standing the concrete was wet. Not with blood, he was pleased to see; the fluid was the colour of bile, and stank to high heaven. Amongst the splashes were several slivers of what might have been human tissue. Evidently Valentin had fought, and succeeded in opening a wound in his attacker. There were more traces of the blood further down the sidewalk, as if the injured thing had crawled some way before taking flight again. With Valentin, presumably. In the face of such strength Harry knew his meagre powers would have availed him not at all, but he felt guilty nevertheless. He'd heard the cry – seen the assailant swoop – and yet fear had sealed his soles to the ground.

He'd last felt fear the equal of this in Wyckoff Street, when Mimi Lomax's demon-lover had finally thrown off any pretence to humanity. The room had filled with the stink of ether and human dirt, and the demon had stood there in its appalling nakedness and shown him scenes that had turned his bowels to water. They were with him now, those scenes. They would be with him forever.

He looked down at the scrap of paper Valentin had given him: the name and address had been rapidly scrawled, but they were just decipherable.

A wise man, Harry reminded himself, would screw this note up and throw it down into the gutter. But if the events in Wyckoff Street had taught him anything, it was that once touched by such malignancy as he had seen and dreamt in the last few hours, there could be no casual disposal of it. He had to follow it to its source, however repugnant that thought was, and make with it whatever bargains the strength of his hand allowed.

160

There was no good time to do business like this: the present would have to suffice. He walked back to Lexington and caught a cab to the address on the paper. He got no response from the bell marked Bernstein, but roused the doorman, and engaged in a frustrating debate with him through the glass door. The man was angry to have been raised at such an hour; Miss Bernstein was not in her apartment, he insisted, and remained untouched even when Harry intimated that there might be some life-or-death urgency in the matter. It was only when he produced his wallet that the fellow displayed the least flicker of concern. Finally, he let Harry in.

'She's not up there,' he said, pocketing the bills. 'She's not been in for days.'

Harry took the elevator: his shins were aching, and his back too. He wanted sleep; bourbon, then sleep. There was no reply at the apartment as the doorman had predicted, but he kept knocking, and calling her.

'Miss Bernstein? Are you there?'

There was no sign of life from within; not at least, until he said:

'I want to talk about Swann.'

He heard an intake of breath, close to the door.

'Is somebody there?' he asked. 'Please answer. There's nothing to be afraid of.'

After several seconds a slurred and melancholy voice murmured: 'Swann's dead.'

At least *she* wasn't, Harry thought. Whatever forces had snatched Valentin away, they had not yet reached this corner of Manhattan. 'May I talk to you?' he requested.

'No,' she replied. Her voice was a candle flame on the verge of extinction.

'Just a few questions, Barbara.'

'I'm in the tiger's belly,' the slow reply came, 'and it doesn't want me to let you in.'

Perhaps they *had* got here before him.

'Can't you reach the door?' he coaxed her. 'It's not so far . . .'

'But it's eaten me,' she said.

'*Try*, Barbara. The tiger won't mind. *Reach*.'

There was silence from the other side of the door, then a shuffling sound. Was she doing as he had requested? It seemed so. He heard her fingers fumbling with the catch.

'That's it,' he encouraged her. 'Can you turn it? Try to turn it.'

At the last instant he thought: suppose she's telling the truth, and there *is* a tiger in there with her? It was too late for retreat, the door was opening. There was no animal in the hallway. Just a woman, and the smell of dirt. She had clearly neither washed nor changed her clothes since fleeing from the theatre. The evening gown she wore was soiled and torn, her skin was grey with grime. He stepped into the apartment. She moved down the hallway away from him, desperate to avoid his touch.

'It's all right,' he said, 'there's no tiger here.'

Her wide eyes were almost empty; what presence roved there was lost to sanity.

'Oh there is,' she said, 'I'm in the tiger. I'm in it forever.'

As he had neither the time nor the skill required to dissuade her from this madness, he decided it was wiser to go with it.

'How did you get there?' he asked her. 'Into the tiger? Was it when you were with Swann?'

She nodded.

'You remember that, do you?'

'Oh yes.'

'What do you remember?'

'There was a sword; it fell. He was picking up –' She stopped and frowned.

'Picking up what?'

She seemed suddenly more distracted than ever. 'How can you hear me,' she wondered, 'when I'm in the tiger? Are you in the tiger too?'

'Maybe I am,' he said, not wanting to analyse the metaphor too closely.

'We're here forever, you know,' she informed him. 'We'll never be let out.'

'Who told you that?'

She didn't reply, but cocked her head a little.

'Can you hear?' she said.

'Hear?'

She took another step back down the hallway. Harry listened, but he could hear nothing. The growing agitation on Barbara's face was sufficient to send him back to the front door and open it, however. The elevator was in operation. He could hear its soft hum across the landing. Worse: the lights in the hallway and on the stairs were deteriorating; the bulbs losing power with every foot the elevator ascended.

He turned back into the apartment and went to take hold of Barbara's wrist. She made no protest. Her eyes were fixed on the doorway through which she seemed to know her judgement would come.

'We'll take the stairs,' he told her, and led her out on to the landing. The lights were within an ace of failing. He glanced up at the floor numbers being ticked off above the elevator doors. Was this the top floor they were on, or one shy of it? He couldn't remember, and there was no time to think before the lights went out entirely.

He stumbled across the unfamiliar territory of the landing with the girl in tow, hoping to God he'd find

163

the stairs before the elevator reached this floor. Barbara wanted to loiter, but he bullied her to pick up her pace. As his foot found the top stair the elevator finished its ascent.

The doors hissed open, and a cold fluorescence washed the landing. He couldn't see its source, nor did he wish to, but its effect was to reveal to the naked eye every stain and blemish, every sign of decay and creeping rot that the paintwork sought to camouflage. The show stole Harry's attention for a moment only, then he took a firmer hold of the woman's hand and they began their descent. Barbara was not interested in escape however, but in events on the landing. Thus occupied she tripped and fell heavily against Harry. The two would have toppled but that he caught hold of the banister. Angered, he turned to her. They were out of sight of the landing, but the light crept down the stairs and washed over Barbara's face. Beneath its uncharitable scrutiny Harry saw decay busy in her. Saw rot in her teeth, and the death in her skin and hair and nails. No doubt he would have appeared much the same to her, were she to have looked, but she was still staring back over her shoulder and up the stairs. The light-source was on the move. Voices accompanied it.

'The door's open,' a woman said.

'What are you waiting for?' a voice replied. It was Butterfield.

Harry held both breath and wrist as the light-source moved again, towards the door presumably, and then was partially eclipsed as it disappeared into the apartment.

'We have to be quick,' he told Barbara. She went with him down three or four steps and then, without warning, her hand leapt for his face, nails opening his cheek. He let go of her hand to protect himself, and in that instant she was away – back up the stairs.

164

He cursed and stumbled in pursuit of her, but her former sluggishness had lifted; she was startlingly nimble. By the dregs of light from the landing he watched her reach the top of the stairs and disappear from sight.

'Here I am,' she called out as she went.

He stood immobile on the stairway, unable to decide whether to go or stay, and so unable to move at all. Ever since Wyckoff Street he'd hated stairs. Momentarily the light from above flared up, throwing the shadows of the banisters across him; then it died again. He put his hand to his face. She had raised weals, but there was little blood. What could he hope from her if he went to her aid? Only more of the same. She was a lost cause.

Even as he despaired of her he heard a sound from round the corner at the head of the stairs; a soft sound that might have been either a footstep or a sigh. Had she escaped their influence after all? Or perhaps not even reached the apartment door, but thought better of it and about-turned? Even as he was weighing up the odds he heard her say:

'Help me . . .' The voice was a ghost of a ghost; but it was indisputably her, and she was in terror.

He reached for his .38, and started up the stairs again. Even before he had turned the corner he felt the nape of his neck itch as his hackles rose.

She was there. But so was the tiger. It stood on the landing, mere feet from Harry, its body humming with latent power. Its eyes were molten; its open maw impossibly large. And there, already in its vast throat, was Barbara. He met her eyes out of the tiger's mouth, and saw a flicker of comprehension in them that was worse than any madness. Then the beast threw its head back and forth to settle its prey in its gut. She had been swallowed whole, apparently. There was no blood on the landing, nor about the tiger's muzzle; only the appalling sight of the girl's face disappearing down the tunnel of the animal's throat.

She loosed a final cry from the belly of the thing, and as it rose it seemed to Harry that the beast attempted a grin. Its face crinkled up grotesquely, the eyes narrowing like those of a laughing Buddha, the lips peeling back to expose a sickle of brilliant teeth. Behind this display the cry was finally hushed. In that instant the tiger leapt.

Harry fired into its devouring bulk and as the shot met its flesh the leer and the maw and the whole striped mass of it unwove in a single beat. Suddenly it was gone, and there was only a drizzle of pastel confetti spiralling down around him. The shot had aroused interest. There were raised voices in one or two of the apartments, and the light that had accompanied Butterfield from the elevator was brightening through the open door of the Bernstein residence. He was almost tempted to stay and see the light-bringer, but discretion bettered his curiosity, and he turned and made his descent, taking the stairs two and three at a time. The confetti tumbled after him, as if it had a life of its own. Barbara's life, perhaps; transformed into paper pieces and tossed away.

He reached the lobby breathless. The doorman was standing there, staring up the stairs vacantly.

'Somebody get shot?' he enquired.

'No,' said Harry, 'eaten.'

As he headed for the door he heard the elevator start to hum as it descended. Perhaps merely a tenant, coming down for a pre-dawn stroll. Perhaps not.

He left the doorman as he had found him, sullen and confused, and made his escape into the street, putting two block lengths between him and the apartment building before he stopped running. They did not bother to come after him. He was beneath their concern, most likely.

So what was he to do now? Valentin was dead, Barbara Bernstein too. He was none the wiser now than he'd been at the outset, except that he'd learned again the lesson he'd been taught in Wyckoff Street: that when dealing with the Gulfs it was wiser never to believe your eyes. The moment you trusted your senses, the moment you believed a tiger to *be* a tiger, you were half theirs.

Not a complicated lesson, but it seemed he had forgotten it, like a fool, and it had taken two deaths to teach it to him afresh. Maybe it would be simpler to have the rule tattooed on the back of his hand, so that he couldn't check the time without being reminded: *Never believe your eyes.*

The principle was still fresh in his mind as he walked back towards his apartment and a man stepped out of the doorway and said:

'Harry.'

It *looked* like Valentin; a wounded Valentin, a Valentin who'd been dismembered and sewn together again by a committee of blind surgeons, but the same man in essence. But then the tiger had looked like a tiger, hadn't it?

'It's me,' he said.

'Oh no,' Harry said. 'Not this time.'

'What are you talking about? *It's Valentin.*'

'So prove it.'

The other man looked puzzled. 'This is no time for games,' he said, 'we're in desperate straits.'

Harry took his .38 from his pocket and pointed at Valentin's chest. 'Prove it or I shoot you,' he said.

'Are you out of your mind?'

'I saw you torn apart.'

167

'Not quite,' said Valentin. His left arm was swathed in makeshift bandaging from fingertip to mid-bicep. 'It was touch and go . . .' he said, '. . . but everything has its Achilles' heel. It's just a question of finding the right spot.'

Harry peered at the man. He wanted to believe that this was indeed Valentin, but it was too incredible to believe that the frail form in front of him could have survived the monstrosity he'd seen on 83rd Street. No; this was another illusion. Like the tiger: paper and malice.

The man broke Harry's train of thought. 'Your steak . . .' he said.

'My steak?'

'You like it almost burned,' Valentin said. 'I protested, remember?'

Harry remembered. 'Go on,' he said.

'And you said you hated the sight of blood. Even if it wasn't your own.'

'Yes,' said Harry. His doubts were lifting. 'That's right.'

'You asked me to prove I'm Valentin. That's the best I can do.' Harry was almost persuaded. 'In God's name,' Valentin said, 'do we have to debate this standing on the street?'

'You'd better come in.'

The apartment was small, but tonight it felt more stifling than ever. Valentin sat himself down with a good view of the door. He refused spirits or first-aid. Harry helped himself to bourbon. He was on his third shot when Valentin finally said:

'We have to go back to the house, Harry.'

'*What?*'

'We have to claim Swann's body before Butterfield.'

'I did my best already. It's not my business any more.'

168

'So you leave Swann to the Pit?' Valentin said.

'*She* doesn't care, why should I?'

'You mean Dorothea? She doesn't know what Swann was involved with. That's why she's so trusting. She has suspicions maybe, but, insofar as it is possible to be guiltless in all of this, she is.' He paused to adjust the position of his injured arm. 'She was a prostitute, you know. I don't suppose she told you that. Swann once said to me he married her because only prostitutes know the value of love.'

Harry let this apparent paradox go.

'Why did she stay with him?' he asked. 'He wasn't exactly faithful, was he?'

'She loved him,' Valentin replied. 'It's not unheard of.'

'And you?'

'Oh I loved him too, in spite of his stupidities. That's why we have to help him. If Butterfield and his associates get their hands on Swann's mortal remains, there'll be all Hell to pay.'

'I know. I got a glimpse at the Bernstein place.'

'What did you see?'

'Something and nothing,' said Harry. 'A tiger, I thought; only it wasn't.'

'The old paraphernalia,' Valentin commented.

'And there was something else with Butterfield. Something that shed light: I didn't see what.'

'The Castrato,' Valentin muttered to himself, clearly discomfited. 'We'll have to be careful.'

He stood up, the movement causing him to wince. 'I think we should be on our way, Harry.'

'Are you paying me for this?' Harry inquired, 'or am I doing it all for love?'

'You're doing it because of what happened at Wyckoff Street,' came the softly-spoken reply. 'Because you lost

169

poor Mimi Lomax to the Gulfs, and you don't want to lose Swann. That is, if you've not already done so.'

They caught a cab on Madison Avenue and headed back uptown to 61st Street, keeping their silence as they rode. Harry had half a hundred questions to ask of Valentin. Who was Butterfield, for one, and what was Swann's crime was that he be pursued to death and beyond? So many puzzles. But Valentin looked sick and unfit for plying with questions. Besides, Harry sensed that the more he knew the less enthusiastic he would be about the journey they were now taking.

'We have perhaps one advantage –' Valentin said as they approached 61st Street. 'They can't be expecting this frontal attack. Butterfield presumes I'm dead, and probably thinks you're hiding your head in mortal terror.'

'I'm working on it.'

'You're not in danger,' Valentin replied, 'at least not the way Swann is. If they were to take you apart limb by limb it would be nothing beside the torments they have waiting for the magician.'

'Illusionist,' Harry corrected him, but Valentin shook his head.

'Magician he was; magician he will always be.'

The driver interrupted before Harry could quote Dorothea on the subject.

'What number you people want?' he said.

'Just drop us here on the right,' Valentin instructed him. 'And wait for us, understand?'

'Sure.'

Valentin turned to Harry. 'Give the man fifty dollars.'

'*Fifty?*'

'Do you want him to wait or not?'

Harry counted four tens and ten singles into the driver's hand.

'You'd better keep the engine running,' he said.

'Anything to oblige,' the driver grinned.

Harry joined Valentin on the sidewalk and they walked the twenty-five yards to the house. The street was still noisy, despite the hour: the party that Harry had seen in preparation half a night ago was at its height. There was no sign of life at the Swann residence however.

Perhaps they *don't* expect us, Harry thought. Certainly this head-on assault was about the most foolhardy tactic imaginable, and as such might catch the enemy off-guard. But were such forces ever off-guard? Was there ever a minute in their maggoty lives when their eyelids drooped and sleep tamed them for a space? No. In Harry's experience it was only the good who needed sleep; iniquity and its practitioners were awake every eager moment, planning fresh felonies.

'How do we get in?' he asked as they stood outside the house.

'I have the key,' Valentin replied, and went to the door.

There was no retreat now. The key was turned, the door was open, and they were stepping out of the comparative safety of the street. The house was as dark within as it had appeared from without. There was no sound of human presence on any of the floors. Was it possible that the defences Swann had laid around his corpse had indeed rebuffed Butterfield, and that he and his cohorts had retreated? Valentin quashed such misplaced optimism almost immediately, taking hold of Harry's arm and leaning close to whisper:

'They're here.'

This was not the time to ask Valentin how he knew, but Harry made a mental note to enquire when, or rather *if*, they got out of the house with their tongues still in their heads.

Valentin was already on the stairs. Harry, his eyes still accustoming themselves to the vestigial light that crept in from the street, crossed the hallway after him. The other man moved confidently in the gloom, and Harry was glad of it. Without Valentin plucking at his sleeve, and guiding him around the half-landing he might well have crippled himself.

Despite what Valentin had said, there was no more sound or sight of occupancy up here than there had been below, but as they advanced towards the master bedroom where Swann lay, a rotten tooth in Harry's lower jaw that had lately been quiescent began to throb afresh, and his bowels ached to break wind. The anticipation was crucifying. He felt a barely suppressible urge to yell out, and to oblige the enemy to show its hand, if indeed it had hands to show.

Valentin had reached the door. He turned his head in Harry's direction, and even in the murk it was apparent that fear was taking its toll on him too. His skin glistened; he stank of fresh sweat.

He pointed towards the door. Harry nodded. He was as ready as he was ever going to be. Valentin reached for the door handle. The sound of the lock-mechanism seemed deafeningly loud, but it brought no response from anywhere in the house. The door swung open, and the heady scent of flowers met them. They had begun to decay in the forced heat of the house; there was a rankness beneath the perfume. More welcome than the scent was the light. The curtains in the room had not been entirely drawn, and the street-lamps described the interior: the flowers massed like clouds around the

172

casket; the chair where Harry had sat, the Calvados bottle beside it; the mirror above the fireplace showing the room its secret self.

Valentin was already moving across to the casket, and Harry heard him sigh as he set eyes on his old master. He wasted little time, but immediately set to lifting the lower half of the casket lid. It defeated his single arm however and Harry went to his assistance, eager to get the job done and be away. Touching the solid wood of the casket brought his nightmare back with breath-snatching force: the Pit opening beneath him, the illusionist rising from his bed like a sleeper unwillingly woken. There was no such spectacle now, however. Indeed a little life in the corpse might have made the job easier. Swann was a big man, and his limp body was uncooperative to a fault. The simple act of lifting him from his casket took all their breath and attention. He came at last, though reluctantly, his long limbs flopping about.

'Now . . .' said Valentin '. . . downstairs.'

As they moved to the door something in the street ignited, or so it seemed, for the interior suddenly brightened. The light was not kind to their burden. It revealed the crudity of the cosmetics applied to Swann's face, and the burgeoning putrescence beneath. Harry had an instant only to appreciate these felicities, and then the light brightened again, and he realised that it wasn't *out*side, but *in*.

He looked up at Valentin, and almost despaired. The luminescence was even less charitable to servant than to master; it seemed to strip the flesh from Valentin's face. Harry caught only a glimpse of what it revealed beneath – events stole his attention an instant later – but he saw enough to know that had Valentin not been his

173

accomplice in this venture he might well have run from him.

'*Get him out of here!*' Valentin yelled.

He let go of Swann's legs, leaving Harry to steer Swann single-handed. The corpse proved recalcitrant however. Harry had only made two cursing steps towards the exit when things took a turn for the cataclysmic.

He heard Valentin unloose an oath, and looked up to see that the mirror had given up all pretence to reflection, and that something was moving up from its liquid depths, bringing the light with it.

'What is it?' Harry breathed.

'The Castrato,' came the reply. 'Will you *go*?'

There was no time to obey Valentin's panicked instruction however, before the hidden thing broke the plane of the mirror and invaded the room. Harry had been wrong. It did not carry the light with it as it came: it *was* the light. Or rather, some holocaust blazed in its bowels, the glare of which escaped through the creature's body by whatever route it could. It had once been human; a mountain of a man with the belly and the breasts of a neolithic Venus. But the fire in its body had twisted it out of true, breaking out through its palms and its navel, burning its mouth and nostrils into one ragged hole. It had, as its name implied, been unsexed; from that hole too, light spilled. By it, the decay of the flowers speeded into seconds. The blossoms withered and died. The room was filled in moments with the stench of rotting vegetable matter.

Harry heard Valentin call his name, once, and again. Only then did he remember the body in his arms. He dragged his eyes from the hovering Castrato, and carried Swann another yard. The door was at his back, and open. He dragged his burden out into the landing as the Castrato kicked over the casket. He heard the din,

174

and then shouts from Valentin. There followed another terrible commotion, and the high-pitched voice of the Castrato, talking through that hole in its face.

'Die and be happy,' it said, and a hail of furniture was flung against the wall with such force chairs embedded themselves in the plaster. Valentin had escaped the assault however, or so it seemed, for an instant later Harry heard the Castrato shriek. It was an appalling sound: pitiful and revolting. He would have stopped his ears, but he had his hands full.

He had almost reached the top of the stairs. Dragging Swann a few steps further he laid the body down. The Castrato's light was not dimmed, despite its complaints; it still flickered on the bedroom wall like a midsummer thunderstorm. For the third time tonight – once on 83rd Street, and again on the stairs of the Bernstein place – Harry hesitated. If he went back to help Valentin perhaps there would be worse sights to see than ever Wyckoff Street had offered. But there could be no retreat this time. Without Valentin he was lost. He raced back down the landing and flung open the door. The air was thick; the lamps rocking. In the middle of the room hung the Castrato, still defying gravity. It had hold of Valentin by his hair. Its other hand was poised, first and middle fingers spread like twin horns, about to stab out its captive's eyes.

Harry pulled his .38 from his pocket, aimed, and fired. He had always been a bad shot when given more than a moment to take aim, but *in extremis*, when instinct governed rational thought, he was not half bad. This was such an occasion. The bullet found the Castrato's neck, and opened another wound. More in surprise than pain perhaps, it let Valentin go. There was a leakage of light from the hole in its neck, and it put its hand to the place.

Valentin was quickly on his feet.

'Again,' he called to Harry. '*Fire again!*'

Harry obeyed the instruction. His second bullet pierced the creature's chest, his third its belly. This last wound seemed particularly traumatic; the distended flesh, ripe for bursting, broke – and the trickle of light that spilled from the wound rapidly became a flood as the abdomen split.

Again the Castrato howled, this time in panic, and lost all control of its flight. It reeled like a pricked balloon towards the ceiling, its fat hands desperately attempting to stem the mutiny in its substance. But it had reached critical mass; there was no making good the damage done. Lumps of its flesh began to break from it. Valentin, either too stunned or too fascinated, stood staring up at the disintegration while rains of cooked meat fell around him. Harry took hold of him and hauled him back towards the door.

The Castrato was finally earning its name, unloosing a desolate ear-piercing note. Harry didn't wait to watch its demise, but slammed the bedroom door as the voice reached an awesome pitch, and the windows smashed.

Valentin was grinning.

'Do you know what we did?' he said.

'Never mind. Let's just get the fuck out of here.'

The sight of Swann's corpse at the top of the stairs seemed to chasten Valentin. Harry instructed him to assist, and he did so as efficiently as his dazed condition allowed. Together they began to escort the illusionist down the stairs. As they reached the front door there was a final shriek from above, as the Castrato came apart at the seams. Then silence.

The commotion had not gone unnoticed. Revellers had appeared from the house opposite, a crowd of

176

late-night pedestrians had assembled on the sidewalk. 'Some party,' one of them said as the trio emerged.

Harry had half expected the cab to have deserted them, but he had reckoned without the driver's curiosity. The man was out of his vehicle and staring up at the first floor window.

'Does he need a hospital?' he asked as they bundled Swann into the back of the cab.

'No,' Harry returned. 'He's about as good as he's going to get.'

'Will you *drive*?' said Valentin.

'Sure. Just tell me where to.'

'Anywhere,' came the weary reply. 'Just get out of here.'

'Hold it a minute,' the driver said, 'I don't want any trouble.'

'Then you'd better *move*,' said Valentin. The driver met his passenger's gaze. Whatever he saw there, his next words were:

'I'm driving,' and they took off along East 61st like the proverbial bat out of hell.

'We did it, Harry,' Valentin said when they'd been travelling for a few minutes. 'We got him back.'

'And that *thing*? Tell me about it.'

'The Castrato? What's to tell? Butterfield must have left it as a watchdog, until he could bring in a technician to decode Swann's defence mechanisms. We were lucky. It was in need of milking. That makes them unstable.'

'How do you know so much about all of this?'

'It's a long story,' said Valentin. 'And not for a cab ride.'

'So what now? We can't drive round in circles all night.'

177

Valentin looked across at the body that sat between them, prey to every whim of the cab's suspension and road-menders' craft. Gently, he put Swann's hands on his lap.

'You're right of course,' he said. 'We have to make arrangements for the cremation, as swiftly as possible.'

The cab bounced across a pot-hole. Valentin's face tightened.

'Are you in pain?' Harry asked him.

'I've been in worse.'

'We could go back to my apartment, and rest there.'

Valentin shook his head. 'Not very clever,' he said, 'it's the first place they'll look.'

'My offices, then –'

'The second place.'

'Well, Jesus, this cab's going to run out of gas eventually.'

At this point the driver intervened.

'Say, did you people mention cremation?'

'Maybe,' Valentin replied.

'Only my brother-in-law's got a funeral business out in Queens.'

'Is that so?' said Harry.

'Very reasonable rates. I can recommend him. No shit.'

'Could you contact him *now*?' Valentin said.

'It's two in the morning.'

'We're in a hurry.'

The driver reached up and adjusted his mirror; he was looking at Swann.

'You don't mind me asking, do you?' he said. 'But is that a body you got back there?'

'It is,' said Harry. 'And he's getting impatient.'

The driver made a whooping sound. 'Shit!' he said. 'I've had a woman drop twins in that seat; I've had whores do business; I even had an alligator back there one time. But this beats them all!' He pondered for a moment, then said: 'You kill him, did you?'

'No,' said Harry.

'Guess we'd be heading for the East River if you had, eh?'

'That's right. We just want a decent cremation. And *quickly*.'

'That's understandable.'

'What's your name?' Harry asked him.

'Winston Jowitt. But everybody calls me Byron. I'm a poet, see? Leastways, I am at weekends.'

'Byron.'

'See, any other driver would be freaked out, right? Finding two guys with a body in the back seat. But the way I see it, it's all material.'

'For the poems.'

'Right,' said Byron. 'The Muse is a fickle mistress. You have to take it where you find it, you know? Speaking of which, you gentlemen got any idea where you want to go?'

'Make it your offices,' Valentin told Harry. 'And he can call his brother-in-law.'

'Good,' said Harry. Then, to Byron:

'Head west along 45th Street to 8th.'

'You got it,' said Byron, and the cab's speed doubled in the space of twenty yards. 'Say,' he said, 'you fellows fancy a poem?'

'Now?' said Harry.

'I like to improvise,' Byron replied. 'Pick a subject. Any subject.'

Valentin hugged his wounded arm close. Quietly, he said: 'How about the end of the world?'

179

'Good subject,' the poet replied, 'just give me a minute or two.'

'So soon?' said Valentin.

They took a circuitous route to the offices, while Byron Jowitt tried a selection of rhymes for Apocalypse. The sleep-walkers were out on 45th Street, in search of one high or another; some sat in the doorways, one lay sprawled across the sidewalk. None of them gave the cab or its occupants more than the briefest perusal. Harry unlocked the front door and he and Byron carried Swann up to the third floor.

The office was home from home: cramped and chaotic. They put Swann in the swivel chair behind the furred coffee cups and the alimony demands heaped on the desk. He looked easily the healthiest of the quartet. Byron was sweating like a bull after the climb; Harry felt – and surely looked – as though he hadn't slept in sixty days; Valentin sat slumped in the clients' chair, so drained of vitality he might have been at death's door.

'You look terrible,' Harry told him.

'No matter,' he said. 'It'll all be done soon.'

Harry turned to Byron. 'How about calling this brother-in-law of yours?'

While Byron set to doing so, Harry returned his attention to Valentin.

'I've got a first-aid box somewhere about,' he said. 'Shall I bandage up that arm?'

'Thank you, but no. Like you, I hate the sight of blood. Especially my own.'

Byron was on the phone, chastising his brother-in-law for his ingratitude. 'What's your beef? I got you a client! I *know* the time, for Christ's sake, but business is business . . .'

180

'Tell him we'll pay double his normal rate,' Valentin said.

'You hear that, Mel? *Twice* your usual fee. So get over here, will you?' He gave the address to his brother-in-law, and put down the receiver. 'He's coming over,' he announced.

'Now?' said Harry.

'Now,' Byron glanced at his watch. 'My belly thinks my throat's cut. How about we eat? You got an all night place near here?'

'There's one a block down from here.'

'You want food?' Byron asked Valentin.

'I don't think so,' he said. He was looking worse by the moment.

'OK,' Byron said to Harry, 'just you and me then. You got ten I could borrow?'

Harry gave him a bill, the keys to the street door and an order for doughnuts and coffee, and Byron went on his way. Only when he'd gone did Harry wish he'd convinced the poet to stave off his hunger pangs a while. The office was distressingly quiet without him: Swann in residence behind the desk, Valentin succumbing to sleep in the other chair. The hush brought to mind another such silence, during that last, awesome night at the Lomax house when Mimi's demon-lover, wounded by Father Hesse, had slipped away into the walls for a while, and left them waiting and waiting, knowing it would come back but not certain of when or how. Six hours they'd sat – Mimi occasionally breaking the silence with laughter or gibberish – and the first Harry had known of its return was the smell of cooking excrement, and Mimi's cry of 'Sodomite!' as Hesse surrendered to an act his faith had too long forbidden him. There had been no more silence then, not for a long space: only Hesse's cries, and Harry's pleas for forgetfulness. They had all gone unanswered.

It seemed he could hear the demon's voice now; its demands, its invitations. But no; it was only Valentin. The man was tossing his head back and forth in sleep, his face knotted up. Suddenly he started from his chair, one word on his lips:

'*Swann!*'

His eyes opened, and as they alighted on the illusionist's body, which was propped in the chair opposite, tears came uncontrollably, wracking him.

'He's dead,' he said, as though in his dream he had forgotten that bitter fact. 'I failed him, D'Amour. That's why he's dead. Because of my negligence.'

'You're doing your best for him now,' Harry said, though he knew the words were poor compensation. 'Nobody could ask for a better friend.'

'I was never his friend,' Valentin said, staring at the corpse with brimming eyes. 'I always hoped he'd one day trust me entirely. But he never did.'

'Why not?'

'He couldn't afford to trust anybody. Not in his situation.' He wiped his cheeks with the back of his hand.

'Maybe,' Harry said, 'it's about time you told me what all this is about.'

'If you want to hear.'

'I want to hear.'

'Very well,' said Valentin. 'Thirty-two years ago, Swann made a bargain with the Gulfs. He agreed to be an ambassador for them if they, in return, gave him magic.'

'*Magic?*'

'The ability to perform miracles. To transform matter. To bewitch souls. Even to drive out God.'

182

'That's a miracle?'

'It's more difficult than you think,' Valentin replied.

'So Swann *was* a genuine magician?'

'Indeed he was.'

'Then why didn't he use his powers?'

'He did,' Valentin replied. 'He used them every night, at every performance.'

Harry was baffled. 'I don't follow.'

'Nothing the Prince of Lies offers to humankind is of the least value,' Valentin said, 'or it wouldn't be offered. Swann didn't know that when he first made his Covenant. But he soon learned. Miracles are useless. Magic is a distraction from the real concerns. It's rhetoric. Melodrama.'

'So what exactly are the real concerns?'

'You should know better than I,' Valentin replied. 'Fellowship, maybe? Curiosity? Certainly it matters not in the least if water can be made into wine, or Lazarus to live another year.'

Harry saw the wisdom of this, but not how it had brought the magician to Broadway. As it was, he didn't need to ask. Valentin had taken up the story afresh. His tears had cleared with the telling; some trace of animation had crept back into his features.

'It didn't take Swann long to realise he'd sold his soul for a mess of pottage,' he explained. 'And when he did he was inconsolable. At least he was for a while. Then he began to contrive a revenge.'

'How?'

'By taking Hell's name in vain. By using the magic which it boasted of as a trivial entertainment, degrading the power of the Gulfs by passing off their wonder-working as mere illusion. It was, you see, an act of heroic perversity. Every time a trick of Swann's was explained away as sleight-of-hand, the Gulfs squirmed.'

'Why didn't they kill him?' Harry said.

'Oh, they tried. Many times. But he had allies. Agents in their camp who warned him of their plots against him. He escaped their retribution for years that way.'

'Until now?'

'Until now,' Valentin sighed. 'He was careless, and so was I. Now he's dead, and the Gulfs are itching for him.'

'I see.'

'But we were not entirely unprepared for this eventuality. He had made his apologies to Heaven; and I dare to hope he's been forgiven his trespasses. Pray that he has. There's more than *his* salvation at stake tonight.'

'Yours too?'

'All of us who loved him are tainted,' Valentin replied, 'but if we can destroy his physical remains before the Gulfs claim them we may yet avoid the consequences of his Covenant.'

'Why did you wait so long? Why didn't you just cremate him the day he died?'

'Their lawyers are not fools. The Covenant specifically proscribes a period of lying-in-state. If we had attempted to ignore that clause his soul would have been forfeited automatically.'

'So when is this period up?'

'Three hours ago, at midnight,' Valentin replied. 'That's why they're so desperate, you see. And so dangerous.'

Another poem came to Byron Jowitt as he ambled back up 8th. Avenue, working his way through a tuna salad sandwich. His Muse was not to be rushed. Poems could take as long as five minutes to be finalised; longer if they involved a double rhyme. He didn't hurry on his journey back to the offices therefore, but wandered in a dreamy sort of mood, turning the lines every which way to make them fit. That way he hoped to arrive back with another finished poem. Two in one night was damn good going.

He had not perfected the final couplet however, by the time he reached the door. Operating on automatic pilot he fumbled in his pocket for the keys D'Amour had loaned him, and let himself in. He was about to close the door again when a woman stepped through the gap, smiling at him. She was a beauty, and Byron, being a poet, was a fool for beauty.

'Please,' she said to him, 'I need your help.'

'What can I do for you?' said Byron through a mouthful of food.

'Do you know a man by the name of D'Amour? Harry D'Amour?'

'Indeed I do. I'm going up to his place right now.'

'Perhaps you could show me the way?' the woman asked him, as Byron closed the door.

'Be my pleasure,' he replied, and led her across the lobby to the bottom of the stairs.

'You know, you're very sweet,' she told him; and Byron melted.

Valentin stood at the window.

'Something wrong?' Harry asked.

'Just a feeling,' Valentin commented. 'I have a suspicion maybe the Devil's in Manhattan.'

'So what's new?'

'That maybe he's coming for us.' As if on cue there was a knock at the door. Harry jumped. 'It's all right,' Valentin said, 'he never knocks.'

Harry went to the door, feeling like a fool.

'Is that you, Byron?' he asked before unlocking it.

'Please,' said a voice he thought he'd never hear again. 'Help me . . .'

185

He opened the door. It was Dorothea, of course. She was colourless as water, and as unpredictable. Even before Harry had invited her across the office threshold a dozen expressions, or hints of such, had crossed her face: anguish, suspicion, terror. And now, as her eyes alighted upon the body of her beloved Swann, relief and gratitude.

'You *do* have him,' she said, stepping into the office.

Harry closed the door. There was a chill from up the stairs.

'Thank God. Thank God.' She took Harry's face in her hands and kissed him lightly on the lips. Only then did she notice Valentin.

She dropped her hands.

'What's *he* doing here?' she asked.

'He's with me. With us.'

She looked doubtful. 'No,' she said.

'We can trust him.'

'I said *no*! Get him out, Harry.' There was a cold fury in her; she shook with it. '*Get him out!*'

Valentin stared at her, glassy-eyed. 'The lady doth protest too much,' he murmured.

Dorothea put her fingers to her lips as if to stifle any further outburst. 'I'm sorry,' she said, turning back to Harry, 'but you must be told what this man is capable of –'

'Without him your husband would still be at the house, Mrs Swann,' Harry pointed out. '*He's* the one you should be grateful to, not me.'

At this, Dorothea's expression softened, through bafflement to a new gentility.

'Oh?' she said. Now she looked back at Valentin. 'I'm sorry. When you ran from the house I assumed some complicity . . .'

'With whom?' Valentin inquired.

She made a tiny shake of her head; then said, 'Your arm. Are you hurt?'

'A minor injury,' he returned.

'I've already tried to get it rebandaged,' Harry said. 'But the bastard's too stubborn.'

'Stubborn I am,' Valentin replied, without inflection.

'But we'll be finished here soon –' said Harry.

Valentin broke in. 'Don't tell her anything,' he snapped.

'I'm just going to explain about the brother-in-law –' Harry said.

'The brother-in-law?' Dorothea said, sitting down. The sigh of her legs crossing was the most enchanting sound Harry had heard in twenty-four hours. 'Oh please tell me about the brother-in-law . . .'

Before Harry could open his mouth to speak, Valentin said: 'It's not her, Harry.'

The words, spoken without a trace of drama, took a few seconds to make sense. Even when they did, their lunacy was self-evident. Here she was in the flesh, perfect in every detail.

'What are you talking about?' Harry said.

'How much more plainly can I say it?' Valentin replied. '*It's not her*. It's a trick. An illusion. They know where we are, and they sent *this* up to spy out our defences.'

Harry would have laughed, but that these accusations were bringing tears to Dorothea's eyes.

'Stop it,' he told Valentin.

'No, Harry. You *think* for a moment. All the traps they've laid, all the beasts they've mustered. You suppose she could have escaped that?' He moved away from the window towards Dorothea. 'Where's Butterfield?' he spat. 'Down the hall, waiting for your signal?'

'Shut up,' said Harry.

'He's scared to come up here himself, isn't he?' Valentin went on. 'Scared of Swann, scared of us, probably, after what we did to his gelding.'

Dorothea looked at Harry. 'Make him stop,' she said.

Harry halted Valentin's advance with a hand on his bony chest.

'You heard the lady,' he said.

'That's no lady,' Valentin replied, his eyes blazing. 'I don't know what it is, but it's no lady.'

Dorothea stood up. 'I came here because I hoped I'd be safe,' she said.

'You *are* safe,' Harry said.

'Not with him around, I'm not,' she replied, looking back at Valentin. 'I think I'd be wiser going.'

Harry touched her arm.

'No,' he told her.

'Mr D'Amour,' she said sweetly, 'you've already earned your fee ten times over. Now I think it's time *I* took responsibility for my husband.'

Harry scanned that mercurial face. There wasn't a trace of deception in it.

'I have a car downstairs,' she said. 'I wonder . . . could you carry him downstairs for me?'

Harry heard a noise like a cornered dog behind him and turned to see Valentin standing beside Swann's corpse. He had picked up the heavy-duty cigarette lighter from the desk, and was flicking it. Sparks came, but no flame.

'What the hell are you doing?' Harry demanded.

Valentin didn't look at the speaker, but at Dorothea.

'She knows,' he said.

He had got the knack of the lighter; the flame flared up.

Dorothea made a small, desperate sound.

'Please don't,' she said.

'We'll all burn with him if necessary,' Valentin said.

'He's insane,' Dorothea's tears had suddenly gone.

'She's right,' Harry told Valentin, 'you're acting like a madman.'

'And you're a fool to fall for a few tears!' came the reply. 'Can't you see that if she takes him we've lost everything we've fought for?'

'Don't listen,' she murmured. 'You know me, Harry. You trust me.'

'What's under that face of yours?' Valentin said. 'What are you? A Coprolite? Homunculus?'

The names meant nothing to Harry. All he knew was the proximity of the woman at her side; her hand laid upon his arm.

'And what about you?' she said to Valentin. Then, more softly, 'why don't you show us your wound?'

She forsook the shelter of Harry's side, and crossed to the desk. The lighter flame guttered at her approach.

'Go on . . .' she said, her voice no louder than a breath. '. . . I *dare* you.'

She glanced round at Harry. 'Ask him, D'Amour,' she said. 'Ask him to show you what he's got hidden under the bandages.'

'What's she talking about?' Harry asked. The glimmer of trepidation in Valentin's eyes was enough to convince Harry there was merit in Dorothea's request. 'Explain,' he said.

Valentin didn't get the chance however. Distracted by Harry's demand he was easy prey when Dorothea reached across the desk and knocked the lighter from his hand. He bent to retrieve it, but she seized on the *ad hoc* bundle of bandaging and pulled. It tore, and fell away.

She stepped back. 'See?' she said.

189

Valentin stood revealed. The creature on 83rd Street had torn the sham of humanity from his arm; the limb beneath was a mass of blue-black scales. Each digit of the blistered hand ended in a nail that opened and closed like a parrot's beak. He made no attempt to conceal the truth. Shame eclipsed every other response.

'I warned you,' she said, 'I warned you he wasn't to be trusted.'

Valentin stared at Harry. 'I have no excuses,' he said. 'I only ask you to believe that I want what's best for Swann.'

'How can you?' Dorothea said. 'You're a demon.'

'More than that,' Valentin replied, 'I'm Swann's Tempter. His familiar; his creature. But I belong to him more than I ever belonged to the Gulfs. And I will defy them –' he looked at Dorothea, '– and their agents.'

She turned to Harry. 'You have a gun,' she said. 'Shoot the filth. You mustn't suffer a thing like that to live.'

Harry looked at the pustulent arm; at the clacking fingernails: what further repugnance was there in wait behind the flesh façade?

'Shoot it,' the woman said.

He took his gun from his pocket. Valentin seemed to have shrunk in the moments since the revelation of his true nature. Now he leaned against the wall, his face slimy with despair.

'Kill me then,' he said to Harry, 'kill me if I revolt you so much. But Harry, I *beg* you, don't give Swann to her. Promise me that. Wait for the driver to come back, and dispose of the body by whatever means you can. Just don't give it to her!'

'Don't listen,' Dorothea said. 'He doesn't care about Swann the way I do.'

Harry raised the gun. Even looking straight at death, Valentin did not flinch.

'You've failed, Judas,' she said to Valentin. 'The magician's mine.'

'What magician?' said Harry.

'Why Swann, of course!' she replied lightly. 'How many magicians have you got up here?'

Harry dropped his bead on Valentin.

'He's an illusionist,' he said, 'you told me that at the very beginning. Never call him a magician, you said.'

'Don't be pedantic,' she replied, trying to laugh off her *faux pas*.

He levelled the gun at her. She threw back her head suddenly, her face contracting, and unloosed a sound of which, had Harry not heard it from a human throat, he would not have believed the larynx capable. It rang down the corridor and the stairs, in search of some waiting ear.

'Butterfield is here,' said Valentin flatly.

Harry nodded. In the same moment she came towards him, her features grotesquely contorted. She was strong and quick; a blur of venom that took him off-guard. He heard Valentin tell him to kill her, before she transformed. It took him a moment to grasp the significance of this, by which time she had her teeth at his throat. One of her hands was a cold vice around his wrist; he sensed strength in her sufficient to powder his bones. His fingers were already numbed by her grip; he had no time to do more than depress the trigger. The gun went off. Her breath on his throat seemed to gush from her. Then she loosed her hold on him, and staggered back. The shot had blown open her abdomen.

He shook to see what he had done. The creature, for all its shriek, still resembled a woman he might have loved.

191

'Good,' said Valentin, as the blood hit the office floor in gouts. 'Now it must show itself.'

Hearing him, she shook her head. 'This is all there is to show,' she said.

Harry threw the gun down. 'My God,' he said softly, 'it's her . . .'

Dorothea grimaced. The blood continued to come. 'Some *part* of her,' she replied.

'Have you always been with them then?' Valentin asked.

'Of course not.'

'Why then?'

'Nowhere to go . . .' she said, her voice fading by the syllable. 'Nothing to believe in. All lies. Everything: *lies*.'

'So you sided with Butterfield?'

'Better Hell,' she said, 'than a false Heaven.'

'Who taught you that?' Harry murmured.

'Who do you think?' she replied, turning her gaze on him. Though her strength was going out of her with the blood, her eyes still blazed. 'You're finished, D'Amour,' she said. 'You, and the demon, and Swann. There's nobody left to help you now.'

Despite the contempt in her words he couldn't stand and watch her bleed to death. Ignoring Valentin's imperative that he keep clear, he went across to her. As he stepped within range she lashed out at him with astonishing force. The blow blinded him a moment; he fell against the tall filing cabinet, which toppled sideways. He and it hit the ground together. *It* spilled papers; he, curses. He was vaguely aware that the woman was moving past him to escape, but he was too busy keeping his head from spinning to prevent her. When equilibrium returned she had gone, leaving her bloody handprints on wall and door.

Chaplin, the janitor, was protective of his territory. The basement of the building was a private domain in which he sorted through office trash, and fed his beloved furnace, and read aloud his favourite passages from the Good Book; all without fear of interruption. His bowels – which were far from healthy – allowed him little slumber. A couple of hours a night, no more, which he supplemented with dozing through the day. It was not so bad. He had the seclusion of the basement to retire to whenever life upstairs became too demanding; and the forced heat would sometimes bring strange waking dreams.

Was this such a dream; this insipid fellow in his fine suit? If not, how had he gained access to the basement, when the door was locked and bolted? He asked no questions of the intruder. Something about the way the man stared at him baffled his tongue. 'Chaplin,' the fellow said, his thin lips barely moving, 'I'd like you to open the furnace.'

In other circumstances he might well have picked up his shovel and clouted the stranger across the head. The furnace was his baby. He knew, as no-one else knew, its quirks and occasional petulance; he loved, as no-one else loved, the roar it gave when it was content; he did not take kindly to the proprietorial tone the man used. But he'd lost the will to resist. He picked up a rag and opened the peeling door, offering its hot heart to this man as Lot had offered his daughters to the stranger in Sodom.

Butterfield smiled at the smell of heat from the furnace. From three floors above he heard the woman crying out for help; and then, a few moments later, a shot. She had failed. He had thought she would. But her life was forfeit anyway. There was no loss in sending her into the breach, in the slim chance that she might have coaxed the body from its keepers. It would have saved the inconvenience of a full-scale attack, but no matter. To have Swann's soul was worth any effort. He had defiled the good name of the Prince of Lies. For that he would suffer as no other miscreant magician ever had. Beside Swann's punishment, Faust's would be an inconvenience, and Napoleon's a pleasure-cruise.

As the echoes of the shot died above, he took the black lacquer box from his jacket pocket. The janitor's eyes were turned heavenward. He too had heard the shot.

'It was nothing,' Butterfield told him. 'Stoke the fire.'

Chaplin obeyed. The heat in the cramped basement rapidly grew. The janitor began to sweat; his visitor did not. He stood mere feet from the open furnace door and gazed into the brightness with impassive features. At last, he seemed satisfied.

'Enough,' he said, and opened the lacquer box. Chaplin thought he glimpsed movement in the box, as though it were full to the lid with maggots, but before he had a chance to look more closely both the box and contents were pitched into the flames.

'Close the door,' Butterfield said. Chaplin obeyed. 'You may watch over them awhile, if it pleases you. They need the heat. It makes them mighty.'

He left the janitor to keep his vigil beside the furnace, and went back up to the hallway. He had left the street door open, and a pusher had come in out of the cold to do business with a client. They bartered in the shadows, until the pusher caught sight of the lawyer.

'Don't mind me,' Butterfield said, and started up the stairs. He found the widow Swann on the first landing.

194

She was not quite dead, but he quickly finished the job D'Amour had started.

'We're in trouble,' said Valentin. 'I hear noises downstairs. Is there any other way out of here?'

Harry sat on the floor, leaning against the toppled cabinet, and tried not to think of Dorothea's face as the bullet found her, or of the creature he was now reduced to needing.

'There's a fire escape,' he said, 'it runs down to the back of the building.'

'Show me,' said Valentin, attempting to haul him to his feet.

'Keep your hands off me!'

Valentin withdrew, bruised by the rebuffal. 'I'm sorry,' he said. 'Maybe I shouldn't hope for your acceptance. But I do.'

Harry said nothing, just got to his feet amongst the litter of reports and photographs. He'd had a dirty life: spying on adulteries for vengeful spouses; dredging gutters for lost children; keeping company with scum because it rose to the top, and the rest just drowned. Could Valentin's soul be much grimier?

'The fire escape's down the hall,' he said.

'We can still get Swann out,' Valentin said. 'Still give him a decent cremation –' The demon's obsession with his master's dignity was chastening, in its way. 'But you have to help me, Harry.'

'I'll help you,' he said, avoiding sight of the creature. 'Just don't expect love and affection.'

If it were possible to hear a smile, that's what he heard.

'They want this over and done with before dawn,' the demon said.

'It can't be far from that now.'

195

'An hour, maybe,' Valentin replied. 'But it's enough. Either way, it's enough.'

The sound of the furnace soothed Chaplin; its rumbles and rattlings were as familiar as the complaint of his own intestines. But there was another sound growing behind the door, the like of which he'd never heard before. His mind made foolish pictures to go with it. Of pigs laughing; of glass and barbed wire being ground between the teeth; of hoofed feet dancing on the door. As the noises grew so did his trepidation, but when he went to the basement door to summon help it was locked; the key had gone. And now, as if matters weren't bad enough, the light went out.

He began to fumble for a prayer –

'Holy Mary, Mother of God, pray for us sinners now and at the hour –'

But he stopped when a voice addressed him, quite clearly.

'Michelmas,' it said.

It was unmistakably his mother. And there could be no doubt of its source, either. It came from the furnace.

'*Michelmas*,' she demanded, 'are you going to let me cook in here?'

It wasn't possible, of course, that she was there in the flesh: she'd been dead thirteen long years. But some phantom, perhaps? He believed in phantoms. Indeed he'd seen them on occasion, coming and going from the cinemas on 42nd Street, arm in arm.

'Open up, Michelmas,' his mother told him, in that special voice she used when she had some treat for him. Like a good child, he approached the door. He had never felt such heat off the furnace as he felt now; he could smell the hairs on his arms wither.

'*Open the door*,' Mother said again. There was no denying her. Despite the searing air, he reached to comply.

'That fucking janitor,' said Harry, giving the sealed fire escape door a vengeful kick. 'This door's supposed to be left unlocked at all times.' He pulled at the chains that were wrapped around the handles. 'We'll have to take the stairs.'

There was a noise from back down the corridor; a roar in the heating system which made the antiquated radiators rattle. At that moment, down in the basement, Michelmas Chaplin was obeying his mother, and opening the furnace door. A scream climbed from below as his face was blasted off. Then, the sound of the basement door being smashed open.

Harry looked at Valentin, his repugnance momentarily forgotten.

'We shan't be taking the stairs,' the demon said.

Bellowings and chatterings and screechings were already on the rise. Whatever had found birth in the basement, it was precocious.

'We have to find something to break down the door,' Valentin said, '*anything*.'

Harry tried to think his way through the adjacent offices, his mind's eye peeled for some tool that would make an impression on either the fire door or the substantial chains which kept it closed. But there was nothing useful: only typewriters and filing cabinets.

'*Think*, man,' said Valentin.

He ransacked his memory. Some heavy-duty instrument was required. A crowbar; a hammer. An axe! There was an agent called Shapiro on the floor below, who exclusively represented porno performers, one of whom had attempted to blow his balls off the month before. She'd failed, but he'd boasted one day on the stairs that he had now purchased the biggest axe he could find, and would happily take the head off any client who attempted an attack upon his person.

The commotion from below was simmering down. The hush was, in its way, more distressing than the din that had preceded it.

'We haven't got much time,' the demon said.

Harry left him at the chained door. 'Can you get Swann?' he said as he ran.

'I'll do my best.'

By the time Harry reached the top of the stairs the last chatterings were dying away; as he began down the flight they ceased altogether. There was no way now to judge how close the enemy were. On the next floor? Round the next corner? He tried not to think of them, but his feverish imagination populated every dirty shadow.

He reached the bottom of the flight without incident, however, and slunk along the darkened second-floor corridor to Shapiro's office. Half way to his destination, he heard a low hiss behind him. He looked over his shoulder, his body itching to run. One of the radiators, heated beyond its limits, had sprung a leak. Steam was escaping from its pipes, and hissing as it went. He let his heart climb down out of his mouth, and then hurried on to the door of Shapiro's office, praying that the man hadn't simply been shooting the breeze with his talk of axes. If so, they were done for. The office was locked, of course, but he elbowed the frosted glass out, and reached through to let himself in, fumbling for the light switch. The walls were plastered with photographs of sex-goddesses. They scarcely claimed Harry's attention; his panic fed upon itself with every heartbeat he spent here. Clumsily he scoured the office, turning furniture

198

over in his impatience. But there was no sign of Shapiro's axe.

Now, another noise from below. It crept up the staircase and along the corridor in search of him – an unearthly cacophony like the one he'd heard on 83rd Street. It set his teeth on edge; the nerve of his rotting molar began to throb afresh. What did the music signal? Their advance?

In desperation he crossed to Shapiro's desk to see if the man had any other item that might be pressed into service, and there tucked out of sight between desk and wall, he found the axe. He pulled it from hiding. As Shapiro had boasted, it was hefty, its weight the first reassurance Harry had felt in too long. He returned to the corridor. The steam from the fractured pipe had thickened. Through its veils it was apparent that the concert had taken on new fervour. The doleful wailing rose and fell, punctuated by some flaccid percussion.

He braved the cloud of steam and hurried to the stairs. As he put his foot on the bottom step the music seemed to catch him by the back of the neck, and whisper: '*Listen*' in his ear. He had no desire to listen; the music was vile. But somehow – while he was distracted by finding the axe – it had wormed its way into his skull. It drained his limbs of strength. In moments the axe began to seem an impossible burden.

'*Come on down*,' the music coaxed him, '*come on down and join the band.*'

Though he tried to form the simple word 'No', the music was gaining influence upon him with every note played. He began to hear melodies in the caterwauling; long circuitous themes that made his blood sluggish and his thoughts idiot. He knew there was no pleasure to be had at the music's source – that it tempted him only to pain and desolation – yet he could not shake its delirium off. His feet began to move to the call of the pipers. He forgot Valentin, Swann and all ambition for escape, and instead began to descend the stairs. The melody became more intricate. He could hear voices now, singing some charmless accompaniment in a language he didn't comprehend. From somewhere above, he heard his name called, but he ignored the summons. The music clutched him close, and now – as he descended the next flight of stairs – the musicians came into view.

They were brighter than he had anticipated, and more various. More baroque in their configurations (the manes, the multiple heads); more particular in their decoration (the suit of flayed faces; the rouged anus); and, his drugged eyes now stung to see, more atrocious in their choice of instruments. Such instruments! Byron was there, his bones sucked clean and drilled with stops, his bladder and lungs teased through slashes in his body as reservoirs for the piper's breath. He was draped, inverted, across the musician's lap, and even now was played upon – the sacs ballooning, the tongueless head giving out a wheezing note. Dorothea was slumped beside him, no less transformed, the strings of her gut made taut between her splinted legs like an obscene lyre; her breasts drummed upon. There were other instruments too, men who had come off the street and fallen prey to the band. Even Chaplin was there, much of his flesh burned away, his rib-cage played upon indifferently well.

'I didn't take you for a music lover,' Butterfield said, drawing upon a cigarette, and smiling in welcome. 'Put down your axe and join us.'

The word *axe* reminded Harry of the weight in his hands, though he couldn't find his way through the bars of music to remember what it signified.

'Don't be afraid,' Butterfield said, 'you're an innocent in this. We hold no grudge against you.'

'Dorothea . . .' he said.

'She was an innocent too,' said the lawyer, 'until we showed her some sights.'

Harry looked at the woman's body; at the terrible changes that they had wrought upon her. Seeing them, a tremor began in him, and something came between him and the music; the imminence of tears blotted it out.

'Put down the axe,' Butterfield told him.

But the sound of the concert could not compete with the grief that was mounting in him. Butterfield seemed to see the change in his eyes; the disgust and anger growing there. He dropped his half-smoked cigarette and signalled for the music-making to stop.

'Must it be death, then?' Butterfield said, but the enquiry was scarcely voiced before Harry started down the last few stairs towards him. He raised the axe and swung it at the lawyer but the blow was misplaced. The blade ploughed the plaster of the wall, missing its target by a foot.

At this eruption of violence the musicians threw down their instruments and began across the lobby, trailing their coats and tails in blood and grease. Harry caught their advance from the corner of his eye. Behind the horde, still rooted in the shadows, was another form, larger than the largest of the mustered demons, from which there now came a thump that might have been that of a vast jack-hammer. He tried to make sense of sound or sight, but could do neither. There was no time for curiosity; the demons were almost upon him.

Butterfield glanced round to encourage their advance, and Harry – catching the moment – swung the axe a second time. The blow caught Butterfield's shoulder; the arm was instantly severed. The lawyer shrieked; blood sprayed the wall. There was no time for a third blow, however. The demons were reaching for him, smiles lethal.

He turned on the stairs, and began up them, taking the steps two, three and four at a time. Butterfield was still shrieking below; from the flight above he heard Valentin calling his name. He had neither time nor breath to answer.

They were on his heels, their ascent a din of grunts and shouts and beating wings. And behind it all, the jack-hammer thumped its way to the bottom of the flight, its noise more intimidating by far than the chatterings of the berserkers at his back. It was in his belly, that thump; in his bowels. Like death's heartbeat, steady and irrevocable.

On the second landing he heard a whirring sound behind him, and half turned to see a human-headed moth the size of a vulture climbing the air towards him. He met it with the axe blade, and hacked it down. There was a cry of excitement from below as the body flapped down the stairs, its wings working like paddles. Harry sped up the remaining flight to where Valentin was standing, listening. It wasn't the chatter he was attending to, nor the cries of the lawyer; it was the jack-hammer.

'They brought the Raparee,' he said.

'I wounded Butterfield –'

'I heard. But that won't stop them.'

'We can still try the door.'

'I think we're too late, my friend.'

'*No!*' said Harry, pushing past Valentin. The demon had given up trying to drag Swann's body to the door, and had laid the magician out in the middle of the

202

corridor, his hands crossed on his chest. In some last mysterious act of reverence he had set folded paper bowls at Swann's head and feet, and laid a tiny origami flower at his lips. Harry lingered only long enough to re-acquaint himself with the sweetness of Swann's expression, and then ran to the door and proceeded to hack at the chains. · It would be a long job. The assault did more damage to the axe than to the steel links. He didn't dare give up, however. This was their only escape route now, other than flinging themselves to their deaths from one of the windows. That he would do, he decided, if the worst came to the worst. Jump and die, rather than be their plaything.

His arms soon became numb with the repeated blows. It was a lost cause; the chain was unimpaired. His despair was further fuelled by a cry from Valentin – a high, weeping call that he could not leave unanswered. He left the fire door and returned past the body of Swann to the head of the stairs.

The demons had Valentin. They swarmed on him like wasps on a sugar stick, tearing him apart. For the briefest of moments he struggled free of their rage, and Harry saw the mask of humanity in rags and the truth glistening bloodily beneath. He was as vile as those besetting him, but Harry went to his aid anyway, as much to wound the demons as to save their prey.

The wielded axe did damage this way and that, sending Valentin's tormentors reeling back down the stairs, limbs lopped, faces opened. They did not all bleed. One sliced belly spilled eggs in thousands, one wounded head gave birth to tiny eels, which fled to the ceiling and hung there by their lips. In the mêlée he lost sight of Valentin. Forgot about him, indeed, until he heard the jack-hammer again, and remembered the broken look on Valentin's face when he'd named the thing. He'd called it the *Raparee*, or something like.

And now, as his memory shaped the word, it came into sight. It shared no trait with its fellows; it had neither wings nor mane nor vanity. It seemed scarcely even to be flesh, but *forged*, an engine that needed only malice to keep its wheels turning.

At its appearance, the rest retreated, leaving Harry at the top of the stairs in a litter of spawn. Its progress was slow, its half dozen limbs moving in oiled and elaborate configurations to pierce the walls of the staircase and so haul itself up. It brought to mind a man on crutches, throwing the sticks ahead of him and levering his weight after, but there was nothing invalid in the thunder of its body; no pain in the white eye that burned in his sickle-head.

Harry thought he had known despair, but he had not. Only now did he taste its ash in his throat. There was only the window left for him. That, and the welcoming ground. He backed away from the top of the stairs, forsaking the axe.

Valentin was in the corridor. He was not dead, as Harry had presumed, but kneeling beside the corpse of Swann, his own body drooling from a hundred wounds. Now he bent close to the magician. Offering his apologies to his dead master, no doubt. But no. There was more to it than that. He had the cigarette lighter in his hand, and was lighting a taper. Then, murmuring some prayer to himself as he went, he lowered the taper to the mouth of the magician. The origami flower caught and flared up. Its flame was oddly bright, and spread with supernatural efficiency across Swann's face and down his body. Valentin hauled himself to his feet, the firelight burnishing his scales. He found enough strength to incline his head to the body as its cremation began, and then his wounds overcame him. He fell backwards, and lay still. Harry watched as the flames mounted. Clearly the body had been sprinkled with gasoline or something similar, for the fire raged up in moments, gold and green.

Suddenly, something took hold of his leg. He looked down to see that a demon, with flesh like ripe raspberries, still had an appetite for him. Its tongue was coiled around Harry's shin; its claws reached for his groin. The assault made him forget the cremation or the Raparee. He bent to tear at the tongue with his bare hands, but its slickness confounded his attempts. He staggered back as the demon climbed his body, its limbs embracing him.

The struggle took them to the ground, and they rolled away from the stairs, along the other arm of the corridor. The struggle was far from uneven; Harry's repugnance was at least the match of the demon's ardour. His torso pressed to the ground, he suddenly remembered the Raparee. Its advance reverberated in every board and wall.

Now it came into sight at the top of the stairs, and turned its slow head towards Swann's funeral pyre. Even from this distance Harry could see that Valentin's last-ditch attempts to destroy his master's body had failed. The fire had scarcely begun to devour the magician. They would have him still.

Eyes on the Raparee, Harry neglected his more intimate enemy, and it thrust a piece of flesh into his mouth. His throat filled up with pungent fluid; he felt himself choking. Opening his mouth he bit down hard upon the organ, severing it. The demon did not cry out, but released sprays of scalding excrement from pores along its back, and disengaged itself. Harry spat its muscle out as the demon crawled away. Then he looked back towards the fire.

All other concerns were forgotten in the face of what he saw.

Swann had stood up.

He was burning from head to foot. His hair, his clothes, his skin. There was no part of him that was not alight. But he was standing, nevertheless, and raising his hands to his audience in welcome.

The Raparee had ceased its advance. It stood a yard or two from Swann, its limbs absolutely still, as if it were mesmerised by this astonishing trick.

Harry saw another figure emerge from the head of the stairs. It was Butterfield. His stump was roughly tied off; a demon supported his lop-sided body.

'Put out the fire,' demanded the lawyer of the Raparee. 'It's not so difficult.'

The creature did not move.

'*Go on*,' said Butterfield. 'It's just a trick of his. He's dead, damn you. It's just conjuring.'

'No,' said Harry.

Butterfield looked his way. The lawyer had always been insipid. Now he was so pale his existence was surely in question.

'What do you know?' he said.

'It's not conjuring,' said Harry. 'It's *magic*.'

Swann seemed to hear the word. His eyelids fluttered open, and he slowly reached into his jacket and with a flourish produced a handkerchief. It too was on fire. It too was unconsumed. As he shook it out tiny bright birds leapt from its folds on humming wings. The Raparee was entranced by this sleight-of-hand. Its gaze followed the illusory birds as they rose and were dispersed, and in that moment the magician stepped forward and embraced the engine.

206

It caught Swann's fire immediately, the flames spreading over its flailing limbs. Though it fought to work itself free of the magician's hold, Swann was not to be denied. He clasped it closer than a long-lost brother, and would not leave it be until the creature began to wither in the heat. Once the decay began it seemed the Raparee was devoured in seconds, but it was difficult to be certain. The moment – as in the best performances – was held suspended. Did it last a minute? Two minutes? Five? Harry would never know. Nor did he care to analyse. Disbelief was for cowards; and doubt a fashion that crippled the spine. He was content to watch – not knowing if Swann lived or died, if birds, fire, corridor or if he himself – Harry D'Amour – were real or illusory.

Finally, the Raparee was gone. Harry got to his feet. Swann was also standing, but his farewell performance was clearly over.

The defeat of the Raparee had bested the courage of the horde. They had fled, leaving Butterfield alone at the top of the stairs.

'This won't be forgotten, or forgiven,' he said to Harry. 'There's no rest for you. Ever. I am your enemy.'

'I hope so,' said Harry.

He looked back towards Swann, leaving Butterfield to his retreat. The magician had laid himself down again. His eyes were closed, his hands replaced on his chest. It was as if he had never moved. But now the fire was showing its true teeth. Swann's flesh began to bubble, his clothes to peel off in smuts and smoke. It took a long while to do the job, but eventually the fire reduced the man to ash.

By that time it was after dawn, but today was Sunday, and Harry knew there would be no visitors to interrupt his labours. He would have time to gather up the remains; to pound the boneshards and put them with the ashes in a carrier bag. Then he would go out and find himself a bridge or a dock, and put Swann into the river.

There was precious little of the magician left once the fire had done its work; and nothing that vaguely resembled a man.

Things came and went away; that was a kind of magic. And in between? Pursuits and conjurings; horrors, guises. The occasional joy.

That there was room for joy; ah! that was magic too.

THE BOOK OF BLOOD (A POSTCRIPT): ON JERUSALEM STREET

WYBURD LOOKED AT the book, and the book looked back. Everything he'd ever been told about the boy was true.

'How did you get in?' McNeal wanted to know. There was neither anger nor trepidation in his voice; only casual curiosity.

'Over the wall,' Wyburd told him.

The book nodded. 'Come to see if the rumours were true?'

'Something like that.'

Amongst connoisseurs of the bizarre, McNeal's story was told in reverential whispers. How the boy had passed himself off as a medium, inventing stories on behalf of the departed for his own profit; and how the dead had finally tired of his mockery, and broken into the living world to exact an immaculate revenge. They had *written* upon him; tattooed their true testaments upon his skin so that he would never again take their grief in vain. They had turned his body into a living book, a book of blood, every inch of which was minutely engraved with their histories.

Wyburd was not a credulous man. He had never quite believed the story – until now. But here was living proof of its veracity, standing before him. There was no part of McNeal's exposed skin which was not itching with tiny words. Though it was four years and more since the ghosts had come for him, the flesh still looked tender, as though the wounds would never entirely heal.

'Have you seen enough?' the boy asked. 'There's more. He's covered from head to foot. Sometimes he wonders if they didn't write on the inside as well.' He sighed. 'Do you want a drink?'

Wyburd nodded. Maybe a throatful of spirits would stop his hands from trembling.

McNeal poured himself a glass of vodka, took a slug from it, then poured a second glass for his guest. As he did so, Wyburd saw that the boy's nape was as densely inscribed as his face and hands, the writing creeping up into his hair. Not even his scalp had escaped the authors' attentions, it seemed.

'Why do you talk about yourself in the third person?' he asked McNeal, as the boy returned with the glass. 'Like you weren't here . . .?'

'The boy?' McNeal said. 'He isn't here. He hasn't been here in a long time.'

He sat down; drank. Wyburd began to feel more than a little uneasy. Was the boy simply mad, or playing some damn-fool game?

The boy swallowed another mouthful of vodka, then asked, matter of factly: 'What's it worth to you?'

Wyburd frowned. 'What's what worth?'

'His skin,' the boy prompted. 'That's what you came for, isn't it?' Wyburd emptied his glass with two swallows, making no reply. McNeal shrugged. 'Everyone has the right to silence,' he said. 'Except for the boy of course. No silence for him.' He looked down at his hand, turning it over to appraise the writing on his palm. 'The stories go on, night and day. Never stop. They tell themselves, you see. They bleed and bleed. You can never hush them; never heal them.'

He *is* mad, Wyburd thought, and somehow the realisation made what he was about to do easier. Better to kill a sick animal than a healthy one.

'There's a road, you know . . .' the boy was saying. He wasn't even looking at his executioner. 'A road the dead go down. He saw it. Dark, strange road, full of people. Not a day gone by when he hasn't . . . hasn't wanted to go back there.'

'Back?' said Wyburd, happy to keep the boy talking. His hand went to his jacket pocket; to the knife. It comforted him in the presence of this lunacy.

'Nothing's enough,' McNeal said. 'Not love. Not music. Nothing.'

Clasping the knife, Wyburd drew it from his pocket. The boy's eyes found the blade, and warmed to the sight.

'You never told him how much it was worth,' he said.

'Two hundred thousand,' Wyburd replied.

'Anyone he knows?'

The assassin shook his head. 'An exile,' he replied. 'In Rio. A collector.'

'Of skins?'

'Of skins.'

The boy put down his glass. He murmured something Wyburd didn't catch. Then, very quietly, he said:

'Be quick, and do it.'

He juddered a little as the knife found his heart, but Wyburd was efficient. The moment had come and gone before the boy even knew it was happening, much less felt it. Then it was all over, for him at least. For Wyburd the real labour was only just beginning. It took him two hours to complete the flaying. When he was finished – the skin folded in fresh linen, and locked in the suitcase he'd brought for that very purpose – he was weary.

Tomorrow he would fly to Rio, he thought as he left the house, and claim the rest of his payment. Then, Florida.

He spent the evening in the small apartment he'd rented for the tedious weeks of surveillance and planning which had preceded this afternoon's work. He was glad to be leaving. He had been lonely here, and anxious with anticipation. Now the job was done, and he could put the time behind him.

He slept well, lulled to sleep by the imagined scent of orange groves.

It was not fruit he smelt when he woke, however, but something savoury. The room was in darkness. He reached to his right, and fumbled for the lamp-switch, but it failed to come on.

Now he heard a heavy slopping sound from across the room. He sat up in bed, narrowing his eyes against the dark, but could see nothing. Swinging his legs over the edge of the bed, he went to stand up.

His first thought was that he'd left the bathroom taps on, and had flooded the apartment. He was knee-deep in warm water. Confounded, he waded towards the door and reached for the main light-switch, flipping it on. It was not water he was standing in. Too cloying, too precious; too red.

He made a cry of disgust, and turned to haul open the door, but it was locked, and there was no key. He beat

212

a panicked fusillade upon the solid wood, and yelled for help. His appeals went unanswered.

Now he turned back into the room, the hot tide eddying about his thighs, and sought out the fountain-head.

The suitcase. It sat where he had left it on the bureau, and bled copiously from every seam; and from the locks; and from around the hinges – as if a hundred atrocities were being committed within its confines, and it could not contain the flood these acts had unleashed.

He watched the blood pouring out in steaming abundance. In the scant seconds since he'd stepped from the bed the pool had deepened by several inches, and still the deluge came.

He tried the bathroom door, but that too was locked and keyless. He tried the windows, but the shutters were immovable. The blood had reached his waist. Much of the furniture was floating. Knowing he was lost unless he attempted some direct action, he pressed through the flood towards the case, and put his hands upon the lid in the hope that he might yet stem the flow. It was a lost cause. At his touch the blood seemed to come with fresh eagerness, threatening to burst the seams.

The stories go on, the boy had said. *They bleed and bleed*. And now he seemed to hear them in his head, those stories. Dozens of voices, each telling some tragic tale. The flood bore him up towards the ceiling. He paddled to keep his chin above the frothy tide, but in minutes there was barely an inch of air left at the top of the room. As even that margin narrowed, he added his own voice to the cacophony, begging for the nightmare to stop. But the other voices drowned him out with their stories, and as he kissed the ceiling his breath ran out.

The dead have highways. They run, unerring lines of ghost-trains, of dream-carriages, across the wasteland behind our lives, bearing an endless traffic of departed souls. They have sign-posts, these highways, and bridges and lay-bys. They have turnpikes and intersections.

It was at one of these intersections that Leon Wyburd caught sight of the man in the red suit. The throng pressed him forward, and it was only when he came closer that he realised his error. The man was not wearing a suit. He was not even wearing his skin. It was not the McNeal boy however; he had gone on from this point long since. It was another flayed man entirely. Leon fell in beside the man as he walked, as they talked together. The flayed man told him how he had come to this condition; of his brother-in-law's conspiracies, and the ingratitude of his daughter. Leon in turn told of his last moments.

It was a great relief to tell the story. Not because he wanted to be remembered, but because the telling relieved him of the tale. It no longer belonged to him, that life, that death. He had better business, as did they all. Roads to travel; splendours to drink down. He felt the landscape widen. Felt the air brightening.

What the boy had said was true. The dead have highways.

Only the living are lost.

☐	Books of Blood Vol 1	Clive Barker	£4.99
☐	Books of Blood Vol 3	Clive Barker	£4.50
☐	Books of Blood Vol 4	Clive Barker	£4.50
☐	Books of Blood Vol 5	Clive Barker	£3.99
☐	Books of Blood 1st Omnibus	Clive Barker	£7.99
☐	Books of Blood 2nd Omnibus	Clive Barker	£5.99
☐	The Damnation Game	Clive Barker	£5.99

Warner Books now offers an exciting range of quality titles by both established and new authors. All of the books in this series are available from:

    Little, Brown and Company (UK),
    P.O. Box 11,
    Falmouth,
    Cornwall TR10 9EN.

Alternatively you may fax your order to the above address. Fax No. 0326 376423.

Payments can be made as follows: cheque, postal order (payable to Little, Brown and Company) or by credit cards, Visa/Access. Do not send cash or currency. UK customers and B.F.P.O. please allow £1.00 for postage and packing for the first book, plus 50p for the second book, plus 30p for each additional book up to a maximum charge of £3.00 (7 books plus).

Overseas customers including Ireland, please allow £2.00 for the first book plus £1.00 for the second book, plus 50p for each additional book.

NAME (Block Letters) ....

....

ADDRESS ....

....

....

☐ I enclose my remittance for _____

☐ I wish to pay by Access/Visa Card

Number ⬚⬚⬚⬚⬚⬚⬚⬚⬚⬚⬚⬚⬚⬚⬚⬚⬚

Card Expiry Date ⬚⬚⬚⬚